Aurora ONE

by

J.M. PHILLIPPE

Blue Zephyr Press
2661 N. Pearl, #360
Tacoma WA 98407

Cover art by **LILT**.

ISBN-10: 1-7320863-2-X
ISBN-13: 978-1-7320863-2-6

Galactic Dreams

What if somewhere out in the future a heroine must save a girl who is already dead?

What if on a planet with no sky a woman with no wings could fly?

What if on a lonely moon there was a prince who could only be rescued by the girl who came to kill him?

Welcome to the universe of Galactic Dreams, where fairy tales are reimagined for a new age—the future. In each Galactic Dreams novella you'll find an old tale reborn with a mixture of romance, technology, aliens and adventure. But beware, a perilous quest awaits behind every star and getting home again will depend on a good spaceship, true love, and maybe just a hint of magic.

Galactic Dreams is a unique series of science-fiction novellas from Blue Zephyr Press featuring retellings of classic tales from different authors, all sharing the same universe, technology, and history.

We hope you enjoy this adventure.

Table of Contents

AURORA ONE

PART I:

The eleventh one had just pronounced her blessing when the thirteenth one suddenly walked in. She wanted to avenge herself for not having been invited, and without greeting anyone or even looking at them she cried out with a loud voice, "In the princess's fifteenth year she shall prick herself with a spindle and fall over dead." And without saying another word she turned around and left the hall. Everyone was horrified, and the twelfth wise woman, who had not yet offered her wish, stepped forward. Because she was unable to undo the wicked wish, but only to soften it, she said, "It shall not be her death. The princess will only fall into a hundred-year deep sleep."

Jacob And Wilhelm Grimm, Little Briar Rose

Chapter 1

Moargan Royal Guard Riska Dvorak felt a drop of sweat run down his spine to the small of his back and resisted the urge to wipe off his forehead. He knew his pale skin was likely flushed red, the freckles on his face popping out more in contrast. There were too many people in the audience chamber, and the atmosphere regulator wasn't doing enough to compensate for the excess body heat. Still he did his best to not fidget while doing his regular visual sweep of the room. His twin sister, Royal Guard Eva Dvorak-Camacho, wasn't having as much luck standing still, and was shifting her weight from foot to foot as though it hurt to stand, her long red braid swinging softly with her movement.

I knew it was too soon for her to come back, he thought. He had pushed back on her request, but she went over his head to Queen Sulina, who had graciously granted her favorite attendant her request. Eva had been very smug about it too. Riska knew Eva had just done it so that she could see all the festivities taking place on the naming day of the royal princess. Her own daughter, Stacia, had her naming day just two weeks before, an intimate celebration of close friends and family. If Riska had his way, that's the kind of affair he would have planned for the princess as well—security at an event like this had been a logistical nightmare. The flower displays and hanging ribbons all seemed designed to create blind spots in his visual field, even if they were pretty. Still, they weren't half as bad as the giant hats and overflowing skirts that many of the guests had chosen to wear. The room was dotted with the colors of all twelve provinces, although the green, blue, and black of Moarga were the most prominent color combo.

Riska told himself that he had taken every precaution that could be taken, despite protestations from the Queen, but he was still nervous he missed something. Being assigned to the princess was a promotion, one he still wasn't quite sure he earned. Still, guarding an infant couldn't be that hard, once the celebrations were over at least.

Riska let his gaze float back over the crowd. He was standing at the edge of a dais centered at one end of the audience chamber. The walls curved out away from the dais, and the floor slanted slightly up the further from the dais it went, all to allow the maximum number of people to view Princess Chavri in her bassinet next to the Queen's chair. It was quite a view, as the princess had taken after her mother with tawny skin and a mass of dark brown hair she had been born with. Her dress in the royal colors of blue, green, and black plaid brought out the green in her hazel eyes. She was a remarkably pretty baby with dark lashes and full pink lips, and her even temper had already won over the crowd. The bassinet had been slightly tilted up, and the sides were lower than usual to also allow maximum view and easy access on the times that the Queen needed to pick her up to present her to some lord. She was sleeping now, despite the sounds and sights all around her, and adorable with her hands fisted up by her face.

The King stood on the Queen's other side and did his best to give a heartfelt speech of thanks for every gift presented to his daughter. A tall man with skin lightly tanned by the sun and thick chestnut hair he kept shorn short, the King made an imposing presence on the dais, the famous Aisling blue eyes sparkling every time he looked at his daughter. The Queen's pride was quieter, revealed in a small smile that never seemed to leave her face. Her beauty had become Chavri's beauty, with the same tawny skin and dark hair and lashes. The Queen's eyes were dark brown though, so dark they almost seemed black, and were all the more striking for it.

Eva was on the King's side of the dais in a position mirroring Riska's and completely in view of the crowd of courtesans filling the room. Eva had asked for that spot specifically, in order to see as many of the gifts as possible. The Queen granted that request as well, liking the symmetry of her two red-headed attendants framing the dais in their matching uniforms of blue and green jackets over black trousers and boots.

Riska bet Eva was regretting her request now though. They were in the third hour of gift presentations, and even his feet were starting to hurt, and he hadn't given birth just over three months ago. Thankfully the delegation from Durrant, the last of the eleven other provinces, was presenting their gifts to the princess, which improbably included a small boat carried in on the shoulders of six of their citizens. What they thought a three-month old was going to do with a boat was beyond Riska, and he looked over and caught his sister's eye to see if she was as amused by this as he was. She was shifting her feet again.

"You're fidgeting, Eva," he said into the microphone in the headpiece hanging off his right ear.

"I'm fine," she said back, and he could see in his peripheral that she was now still.

"It's almost over," he said. "You've handled it like a champ."

"I am a professional," she chided. "Don't think that mother-hood has changed that. And I can still kick your arse. Probably."

Riska chuckled, and heard matching chuckling from various others stationed around the room. It was an open line, but the group was used to the Dvorak twins chatting along it.

"I'd bet on her," Mel said, managing to hide the fact he was speaking by putting a hand in front of his mouth. As the King's dedicated guard, he was standing on the dais, slightly behind and to the right of King Ardan.

"I'll take that wager," Nora chimed in from her position be-hind Queen Sulina's chair. "If anything, motherhood will give Eva an edge." She was speaking from personal experience, hav-ing birthed a child two years ago who had been the darling of the royal guards until Eva's little Stacia came along to bask in the shared attention.

"What do you say, Eva, when should this go down? After dessert?" Riska glanced sideways at his sister and tried to keep himself from smiling. Guards weren't supposed to show any emotion.

But Eva's attention was caught on something else, something that Riska couldn't see. Riska tried to follow where her eyes were looking, but the damn boat was blocking him.

"Eva?" he asked.

"A movement. Something." Her voice was tense.

Riska turned his attention to the crowd's feet on the other side of the boat, looking for any change in their general movement or other sign that something was amiss. There: a set of shoes darker and heavier than the others around them. Riska moved his gaze back to his side of the room and found at least three other pairs of shoes as dark and heavy as the first. They were just shoes, part of his brain told him, but his hand moved to the plasma gun at his side, and his instinct knew that something was definitely wrong.

"Look for dark boots," he said, keeping his tone low so that only other guards could hear him. "Thick heeled. Outside wear. Black or brown."

He was riding a fine line between acting appropriately and overacting, and the last thing he wanted was to create panic in the room and cause some sort of stampede.

"I've got eyes on two sets," he heard Eva say through his ear piece.

"Three up by the Mehmtok contingent," Nora said.

"Two more near the folks from Durrant," Mel added.

The sweat that had been pooling at the base of Riska's spine seemed to turn to ice. He pulled his gun and instinctively jumped up on the dais, moving swiftly toward the princess.

"Alpha response!" he shouted, every instinct in him telling him to get to the princess as soon as possible. The guards positioned throughout the chamber immediately jumped into action, pulling guns and looking for trouble. The mysterious boot-wearing folks threw off cloaks and revealed weapons underneath, and people throughout the chamber screamed and tried to head for the double doors in the back.

Just then, a hand-sized cylinder came soaring out of the crowd, arching down toward Chavri's bassinet. Riska realized with horror that it would land before he could get to it, and he pushed his legs to move faster. He saw Mel drag the King from his chair and away from the bassinet, while Nora had a harder time pulling the Queen away due to her awkward position in the chair between the King's and the bassinet.

The canister bounced off the edge of the bassinet, landing somewhere inside and expelling green gas. Riska took in a deep breath and held it as he lunged forward. The canister was lying next to Chavri's feet, the number thirteen engraved on the metal, and he reached in and grabbed it. His hand instantly felt like it was on fire, but still he kept his grip, pulling the canister out of the bassinet and flinging it to the other side of the dais where the least number of people seemed to be. In the next moment, he swept the princess up in his arms, noting that Nora finally had the Queen pulled away, and that Eva was waving people back from the canister, which was still smoldering and expelling gas.

Riska held Chavri tight to his chest and ran toward the back of the dais, protecting her with his body. Her screams were muffled against his shirt, but he took comfort that at least she was still breathing. He didn't stop until he had her safely ensconced in the reinforced throne room, a force field barrier and a line of guards between the royal family and anyone that would attempt to attack them. Riska looked down at the princess. She was still crying, which was a good sign, but her color was too pale, and there was a tinge of green around her mouth and nose.

Her doctor snatched her from his hands, and Riska finally let go of his breath, taking in deep gulps of air after his run. He saw then that the Queen had collapsed on a small couch and was coughing and choking, her own mouth slightly green, a doctor running a scanning instrument over her. Only the King seemed untouched by the gas, but his guard Mel was on the floor, vomiting violently. Riska looked down at his burned hand, and saw that the flesh looked sick, like it was necrotic. The number thirteen was burned into his flesh.

Eva! The last time he had seen her she was waving people away from the canister, the same one that burned him, the same one that he threw—toward her side of the dais. He pushed past the nurse who was trying to scan his hand and shouldered a few other guards away until he got to the force field.

Nora, the queen's bodyguard, stood between him and the controls.

"You can't," she said. "We have to keep the seal."

"Eva's out there," he said. "I need to get to her. I left her out there. I left…"

"You saved the princess. You did your job. And Eva did hers."

He tried to push past her again, but Nora stood firm.

"I have to get to her," he said again. "I have to…"

But there was something about the way Nora was standing, the sadness in her eyes.

Nora put her hands on Riska's shoulders then, forcing him to look her in the eye.

"She did her job. She saved the royal family. She saved a lot of people. I need to you to hear me. I need you to understand. She did her job."

Riska blinked at Nora several times, cradling his burned hand to his chest.

"She did her job," he repeated, still not fully understanding what Nora was saying.

"She did her job," Nora said back, softly. Then Riska finally understood. He collapsed hard on his knees so suddenly that Nora had no chance to hold him up, and fell to her knees with him.

"No," he said, shaking his head. "No, she...no. She has a baby. Little Stacia. No."

Nora nodded, keeping her hands steady on Riska's shoulders.

"She did her job," she said again. "I saw her do it. She just threw herself down on the canister, covering it with her body. She didn't hesitate. She didn't falter. She did her job."

For a second hope bloomed in Riska's chest.

"Then she might be, she might..."

Nora shook her head, her eyes directing Riska to the proof in the room: Mel, who was still vomiting, the Queen, who was being rushed away on a stretcher, and even Riska's own burned and dead-feeling hand. If Eva had thrown herself on the canister, she wasn't going to survive the experience.

"I'm so sorry," Nora said.

Riska felt it then—the burns, the fear, the adrenaline, and the grief, all at once. His shoulders shook and his head fell forward, heavy tears streaming down his face as he wailed.

PART II:

The Princess

The wise women's gifts were all fulfilled on the girl, for she was so beautiful, well behaved, friendly, and intelligent that everyone who saw her had to love her.

Jacob and Wilhelm Grimm, Little Briar Rose

Chapter 2

Chavri Aisling stared hard at her hand-held and tried not to get too excited. Stacia's message said that scans had detected what could be a metal source in the Kuntak Asteroid Belt, a relatively volatile and under-explored part of their solar system. The astronaut in Chavri was thrilled at the prospect of discovering something new in the space around their planet, while the king's daughter in her was excited by the idea that her province could have a win they sorely needed. Moarga had invested significantly more into space exploration than any other province on L'Mondeau, and while it had cost them a lot—including two space ships, a staggering loss on a planet that didn't have the resources to produce more—they had gained very little from it. Chavri's father, King Ardan, had even been contemplating shutting the space program down. Chavri was desperate to keep it going, not only because of her own love of being in space, but because she firmly believed the best thing for L'Mondeau would be to get back to the stars its people had come from.

A delicate cough to Chavri's right forced her attention away from her hand-held and back toward the ambassador standing just below the dais she and her parents were sitting on. He was giving an impassioned speech about, of all things, potatoes. The ambassador was from Mehmtok, medium height and build, and nothing particular to look at. He wasn't much older than Chavri and obviously very knowledgeable about his topic. He routinely seemed to glance her way, and then swallow visibly, and she wasn't sure what about her was making him nervous. Surely everyone had become accustomed to the sight of the princess and her veils. When he followed up one of his pointed looks with a smile aimed very directly in her direction, Chavri began to sense another reason for his looks, and felt her face start to burn in response.

He was flirting with her. In front of her parents. And the entire court.

Chavri stared at her mother and tried harder to read her face, to see if she could catch any look that might betray some ulterior motive for Chavri being in attendance. The truth was she was rarely asked to perform this type of duty, giving audience to guests of the province. She had thought her parents made an exception this time because the delegation was from Mehmtok, and relations with that province had been strained. Chavri examined the visitor more closely, trying to determine his rank and position in the delegation. If she'd been paying any attention to his introduction, she would know this of course, but her thoughts had been elsewhere at the time. Now she noticed just how fine his shoes were, and the quality and number of chains he wore around his neck. Mehmtok didn't have royalty the way Moarga did, instead being ruled by a group of wealthy merchants. But some of those merchant families had been in power for generations, and the children of those houses often were treated as royalty. Which meant being married off to one of the children of the merchant houses wasn't outside the realm of possibilities.

Oh gods, Chavri thought. *I hope that's not what's happening.*

A vibration from her hand-held indicated another message from Stacia, and Chavri tried very hard not to look down and read it.

She probably never should have had her hand-held with her, but she'd been waiting for news about the scans all day. In truth, she had been waiting to hear from Stacia all day. Stacia had been hard to pin down lately, always seeming to have somewhere else to be when Chavri tried to spend time with her. It had been more than frustrating—it had made Chavri feel even lonelier than usual.

Chavri pulled her *dupatta* away from her face as much as the force-field sealing it to her shoulders would allow, and tried to get a better look at the visitor. Images through the veil were not clear, of course. Everything had a slightly blurred effect, both from looking through a fabric and from the field contained within it.

The potato man was wearing a mask over his mouth and nose, as was the custom for anyone visiting the Moargan palace, the cloth richly embroidered in gold and silver thread. Still, it managed to look more like a surgical mask and less like a piece of clothing. It reminded Chavri of her childhood, and all the masks everyone around her would wear before a little research discovered that her mother's people used to wear *dupatta* back on Earth. The veils could be worn lots of ways, including the way Chavri wore hers, covering her entire face and hair.

Supposedly they were worn by women after marriage for modesty's sake. Modesty was all well and good, but Chavri's *dupatta* was engineered to act as a bio-mask to prevent exposure to any foreign germs. Still, seeing the Mehmtokian's mask was a nice reminder that the veils were definitely an improvement over how things used to be, the kind of things she and others used to have to wear.

All to keep the princess of Moarga safe.

Surely it wouldn't be safe for her to be married. She tried to picture what married life while wearing a mask might be like, particularly since even when wearing her *dupatta* people were made to stand at least an arm's-length away from her. Obviously copulation of any kind would be out of the question—at just over twenty years old, Chavri had never even kissed anyone. Children, her doctors had already told her, were definitely out of the question.

What even would be the point?

Except that the merchant would get a royal title and her province would get much needed wealth. Chavri hoped that Moarga wasn't as bad off as that. Not yet anyway. And not if she had anything to do about it.

Generations ago, the original colony ship that brought them to this planet crash-landed. It had gone off course due to various system failures no one could explain the causes of, and they named the planet after that ship. While the planet proved to be habitable enough for Chavri's people to flourish in areas like agriculture, art, and architecture, the only metals strong enough to withstand entry into or out of the atmosphere came from the ship they landed in. So they stripped it down, every scrap, every bolt, and every wire. Many metal resources went to other things like weapons and tools, but the early leaders of L'Mondeau—at the insistence of Mackenzie Aisling, who would go on to found and rule Moarga as its first king—put aside resources to build spaceships as well so that the colonists could eventually reconnect with the other Earth colonies. King Mackenzie specifically wanted to make contact with their sister colony ship, the Oster, as his brothers were on board. Over the years, many of the first L'Mondeau ships had been lost, and now there were only a half a dozen that could even make the trip in and out of the atmosphere. Chavri had access to one, a small ship called the *Aurora Three* which was named after its two predecessors. That ship and the work she did on it gave meaning to her otherwise hard life.

Chavri couldn't resist the urge anymore and tried to sneak another look at her hand-held, which she thought was hidden discreetly enough in her lap. But her mother caught her at it again and coughed another delicate little cough. Despite the distance the sound had to cover, it had the same effect on Chavri as a leash pulling back a dog, and again she snapped her attention to the Mehmtokian. His speech was painfully boring though, and she found herself pulling at her veil again.

It felt unusually warm in the audience chamber, and Chavri was having trouble breathing easily. She was sure she was sweating, but there was no way to touch her face while the veil she wore was sealed against her clothing, and she dared not unseal it just to wipe her brow. That would defeat the purpose of wearing it in the first place.

Despite the force field keeping the space she, her parents, and their attendants were in separate from any guests, her veil acted as another layer of protection. This one was new, a special gift from the delegation from Mehmtok. It was a light blue-violet with silver-looking fringe and amethyst-colored beading along her forehead, as much to ensure the veil would stay in place as for decoration. It felt rich to her, likely too rich and worth more than what most families in Moarga made in a year. The light color of her veil complimented the light hazel of Chavri's eyes, and the material flowed easily over her carefully braided dark brown hair. She had been wearing some version of the same thing since her confirmation almost ten years ago. She had been told that her *dupatta* was a marvel of technology, a type of cloth that could provide the perfect barrier of a gas mask while still giving the appearance of draped fabric. The force field that formed along the weave of the cloth worked as a bio-filter, ensuring that Chavri never actually breathed the same air as anyone else. Her air was always cleaner, more sterile, and safer.

And yet, for all that, it was also tremendously stifling. Chavri pulled at the fabric-that-was-more-than-fabric again. The force-field resisted her tug, and she only got the slightest bit of room between her face and the folds of cloth, not enough to create a breeze.

Her mother didn't have this problem, as she only wore a half-veil across her nose and mouth, and hers was not sealed with a force-field but tied lightly around her head. Her mother's veil was a transparent light blue, and Chavri imagined her mother could feel a breeze through the fabric, though she had no way of knowing if that was true. The beading in her veil matched the beading of her *Punjabi* suit made in the royal blue and greens. The fabric of the veil had been treated of course—all the veils and masks of those who ever shared space with Chavri had specially treated material to cover their mouths and noses with and work as a low-grade filter so that whatever germs were breathed out didn't make it into the air. "You can never be too careful," seemed to be the unofficial Moargan motto.

Her father's veil wrapped around his head and draped down over his shoulders in a single sash across his chest that was long enough to be tucked into a large belt that gave the impression of a short skirt over his trousers. It was styled in the blue, green, and black plaid of the Aisling clan back on Earth, the part covering his mouth opaque. The blue in his wrap matched the blue of his eyes.

She thought he looked noble in his veil, as her mother looked beautiful in hers. Chavri, who was forced to wear a *gagra choli* with her midriff exposed, did not feel either noble or beautiful, but sweaty and bored.

After a few more moments she began to feel lightheaded, and it was getting harder and harder to not visibly pant. Chavri pulled at her *dupatta* again. It felt almost as if something was sucking the air away from her, and she felt herself start to choke.

Her mother turned to look at Chavri, this time shooting daggers with her eyes before their shape turned to one of acute alarm.

"What's wrong?" she demanded. Her question cut the Mehmtokian's speech off.

Chavri shook her head and focused on her breath. She tried to pull air into her lungs, but there seemed to be no air to pull in. The cloth of her *dupatta* lay flat against her face and pulling and tugging at it couldn't get it to move.

"She's having trouble breathing!" Riska called from his place on the edge of the dais. He became a blur of movements at the edge of her vision, and Chavri kept pulling on the fabric, but couldn't get enough breath to speak.

For a terrible moment, it seemed that no one knew what to do. Chavri could feel her mother hovering just outside of touching range, while her father stood towering above, also frozen in action. Neither could dare approach her, despite every instinct in them telling them to. In fact, no one approached her, out of fear and habit.

And still, it was getting harder and harder to breathe. Soon Chavri was on her knees, yanking forcefully against her veil.

"Don't!" Sulina called. Chavri knew her mother was certain that Chavri taking off her *dupatta* meant certain death, but the panic in Chavri was greater than that certainty. She pulled and yanked at the veil, pressing the button that should release the field over and over again, to no avail. She could feel her chest constrict, her lungs try to take in air that wasn't there.

She heard shouting all around her, but she could no longer make out the words. For long painful moments she pulled and yanked and tried to breathe until it was all she could think about doing. Her hands were all she could see, and even those were starting to fade from view, strength being robbed from them along with the breaths she wasn't able to take.

She felt a powerful force barrel into her and knock her flat just as her vision began to dim. A completely masked face was staring down at her, holding something in its gloved hand. Her first thought was that it was another assassin, trying to kill her. But despite all her training, she could take no move against him as he slashed down with his energy-blade.

Suddenly, there was no veil over her nose and mouth, and the man's gloved hands shoved it off the rest of her face. In some instinct she didn't know she had, Chavri took in a huge gulp of air, and then another, and then another, while the man above her pulled out an instrument and waved it over her. It took her several breaths before she realized that the man in the containment suit was talking to her and telling her over and over again that she was going to be all right.

"I'm here with you," he said. "You're not alone."

He was also wearing a veil over his mouth and nose under his helmet-like mask, and it was this detail that made her finally recognize him: Riska.

Her bodyguard had saved her life. Again.

He then pulled another mask over to her, this one attached to some sort of tank, and while Chavri wanted very badly to push that one away too, she allowed it to be pressed to her face, and took in the clean air.

But when she looked up, she saw that her mother's face was still stricken, and her father was still frozen in fear.

She had been exposed to regular, everyday air, and whatever particles might be floating in it.

And those particles could still kill her.

Chapter 3

Chavri was back in her bubble, as she called it, the hermetically sealed room that she was put in for medical tests and appointments. It didn't look or feel like a medical room though, the bed covered in rich linens, thick drapes on the sealed window, and gorgeous wood floors and carved furnishings. The only real difference between this room and her bedroom was that this one had an observation room attached, one wall given over to a giant glass pane that allowed her to see out and others to see in. The room also had a station near the window with a mechanical arm that could be controlled to take her blood, administer shots, or record her vitals. That, and the complete lack of any personal touch, like books or art work, reminded her that this was a hospital room and not a real bedroom.

"Any news?" she asked Stacia, who was standing in the observation room, fidgeting with the edges of her veil.

Stacia Dvorak-Camacho was short. It wasn't so much a descriptor of her as it was a reality she constantly had to live with. She wore heeled shoes with thick platforms on the soles and bright colors in order to stand out and not be overlooked. She matched her voice to her clothes, making it loud and deep to give her words a sense of gravity her stature didn't have. Her dark brown eyes and hair at least served to give her features a depth they might not otherwise have had, and she highlighted the yellow undertones of her skin with a minimal cosmetic touch, wearing a translucent veil over her mouth and nose in her quest to be as seen as possible.

Today's veil was a pale yellow that contrasted nicely with Stacia's light brown skin, and made her eyes seem even darker brown, ringed with thick black lashes. As pretty as it was, Chavri was a little disappointed that Stacia wore a veil at all. Since Chavri was behind glass and speaking through a sound system, there was no need for anyone to be veiled in her presence. She hoped Stacia was wearing one out of habit and not for any other reason. Chavri felt there had been a lot of barriers between them lately.

"A confirmed false positive," Stacia said, but there was something about the way she said it that made Chavri frown in thought. "We're going to scan in other areas now. What about you—any news on when you might get out of there?"

It was Chavri's turn to shake her head, while also wondering why Stacia was rushing on from the subject Chavri most wanted to talk about. Chavri, Stacia, and Chavri's guard and pilot Lysa Hanna all worked together to scan the solar system around L'Mondeau in search of two things: metal sources that could be mined, and the lost ship *Aurora One*—the first Moargan space ship which had gone missing almost three hundred years ago. Stacia had last reported that she had a potentially strong lead. It was beyond strange that she was now saying it was a false positive, and it left Chavri feeling like she was missing out on something.

This whole visit had been rushed from the beginning, and Chavri was trying not to feel too hurt by it. Probably there was a good reason. Maybe she would even get to hear it at some point.

"There are no signs of infection yet, but the docs have been in a wait-and-see pattern. They keep taking my blood, urine—everything—looking for any sign of illness, and they are keeping me in quarantine for the time being."

"And any word on the…other thing?"

Stacia was right to disguise her meaning. Both she and Chavri knew that all their interactions in this room were being monitored. The overall paranoia of everyone in the palace had dramatically increased since the day Chavri's *dupatta* decided to suck air away from Chavri instead of filter the air that she needed to breathe.

"Everything is still…" Chavri paused, trying to find the right word. "Inconclusive," she settled on at last.

"That sounds fun."

Chavri grinned back.

"Super. This isn't going to impact my life at all."

"Can't see how it possibly could," Stacia agreed. "Who needs freedom anyway?"

Chavri might have laughed if the whole thing wasn't depressing. Thanks to her illness, her movement was already constricted. If this was what everyone feared it could be—another assassination attempt—she wasn't sure her parents would ever let her out of her bubble. And it wasn't as though they didn't have reason to worry. The truth was that the smallest cold could kill Chavri because her body had no way of fighting even the most basic of germs off since it was too busy trying to fight itself.

It was an overly simplistic explanation, but one that Chavri favored. She felt at one with her immune system when she pictured it armed and ready for battle, charging at her bones and muscle and tissue. Only medicine kept it at bay, medicine that interfered with her ability to fight off any other infection. Her mind too was often at odds with itself. In that moment, she wanted to push Stacia more on the scans and the supposed false positive, while also recognizing that it was probably the last thing she should do. But this was always her life—trying to find a balance between her wants and her shoulds.

"I'm glad you're all right," Stacia said, her voice unusually solemn. "I was really worried." She looked down then, her hands fidgeting with her veil edge in an uncharacteristically anxious matter.

"I really am," Chavri said. "I mean, still isolated and locked away and all that, but you know, nothing worse than usual." She tried to laugh off her comment, but her chuckle came out flat and bitter.

"It won't always be like this," Stacia said.

"I don't see how. It's been almost twenty years, and the doctors still don't have a cure. Gods, they barely have an improved treatment."

"I have faith," Stacia said, smiling at Chavri. It was the kind of smile that demanded a smile in return, and Chavri felt lighter for seeing it, and felt the distance between them shrink. If only there wasn't an actual barrier, too.

"I'm really glad you came," she said.

"Always."

Chavri wanted to say something else, but couldn't think of anything to say. So she just stared at Stacia until the moment seemed to stretch longer than was comfortable.

Fortunately it was broken by the sound of the door to the observation room opening.

"Visiting time is over," Riska said, striding in. Riska was wearing his usual plain, opaque, dark gray veil carefully arranged over half his face and tucked into his tunic. Dark blue eyes stared somberly over the veil, thick reddish brows still and unexpressive. He considered his veil part of his uniform and Chavri had never seen him without it. Stacia swore she'd never seen him without it either, but Chavri assumed she had to be lying about that, since Riska was her uncle. Surely he didn't wear his veil around family.

"We have more time," Chavri protested, looking at her chronometer.

"Your parents need to see you," Riska said. This earned a raised eyebrow from Stacia, and a deeper frown from Chavri.

"I'll see you soon," Stacia promised.

"Hopefully with better news," Chavri said. Stacia just smiled back.

"May the gods hold you, Uncle," she said to Riska her way out.

"May the gods hold you," he responded.

Chavri's eyes followed her friend with some small concern. Something was definitely up with Stacia, and she wished she knew what it was. She wished they had more time together. She wished…. But it didn't do to spend her time wishing.

She turned her attention to Riska.

"Any idea when I will be able to get out of here?" Chavri asked.

Riska shook his head.

"It's not my place to say."

"But you know something, even if you won't say what it is."

"Your parents will speak with you." He turned and walked back to his post outside the door to the observation room, probably to make whatever preparations were necessary for their visit.

Chavri sighed. She'd never been able to get anything from Riska, except extra cakes, which he'd snuck to her when she was little, his expression never changing when she found them on the table just outside her room. He was kind, just a stickler for the rules.

Chavri had time to grow restless enough to pace back and forth before the door to the observation room opened again and her parents and their dedicated personal guard came in. While the guard wore veils, her parents did not, and it was almost startling to see their faces without any barriers between them. Her father had more lines around his mouth than she remembered, but her mother's face looked unchanged and as beautiful as ever.

"Darling," her mother said. "You look well!"

"I feel well," Chavri said.

"The doctors can find no trace of illness," her father said. "You were very lucky." He didn't smile, despite the good news of his statement and crossed his arms across his chest in a pose that Chavri knew all too well. It meant he was going to tell her something she wasn't going to want to hear.

"But we're still not sure what caused your *dupatta* to malfunction the way it did."

This was not good news, and opened up the worst case scenario.

"The Thirteenth?" she asked.

The Thirteenth attacked Chavri on her naming day and killed

three guards including Stacia's mother. Their poison had caused the Queen to become infertile and had left Chavri cursed to a life behind masks. They were a collective of radical zealots who were trying to carve out a thirteenth province on L'Mondeau and who held disdain for science, particularly anything to do with space flight. The Thirteenth believed that the original colonists should never have left Earth in the first place. They were part of the Naturalist movement that emerged after Earth—and the newly founded Interplanetary Alliance—began to send out colony ships *en masse*. The main tenet of Naturalism stated that neither people nor planets should be modified. Gene editing and cybernetics were considered heresy and planets were to be left mostly uninhabited and as natural as possible. All the modifications that the various provinces of L'Mondeau had made to the planet in order to live were seen as anathema.

The Thirteenth had some territory in the Harbin Mountains, in between the Moarga and Mehmtok provinces, that were too remote or uninhabitable to otherwise be claimed and had been fighting for recognition off and on for over two generations. Their specialty was biochemical warfare, and over the past several years, their attacks were getting more frequent and aimed at larger targets.

Technical sabotage was a new tactic, and if The Thirteenth really were responsible for the malfunction of Chavri's *dupatta*, it left Chavri concerned about her parents' reaction.

"I'm not staying in here," Chavri started, and her mother put up a hand as though to ward off the rest of Chavri's rant.

"No one is saying that," she began. "You will be allowed to

return to your regular chambers."

"But." Chavri waited. Her father sighed.

"We don't like this anymore than you do. I promise you, it is not our intention to make your life miserable. We just want to keep you safe."

"Something that your condition makes…just a little more challenging." Her mother smiled brightly at her. They shared the same dark hair and tawny skin, though Chavri's eyes were much lighter than her mother's. Still, Chavri could recognize the smile on her mother's face as being the twin of the one Chavri put on when greeting officials from other provinces. It had a forced feel to it that robbed it of genuine warmth.

"I am not giving up my work," Chavri said, crossing her own arms in a mirror to her father's pose.

"No one is saying that."

He stared hard back at her.

"Just tell me. What are my new restrictions?"

"We're not sure your *dupatta* are safe anymore," her mother said, her eyes filled with real sympathy. "We can turn the room that you're in now into a work room."

"My work is with Stacia and Lysa. In the lab. Which is a sealed room—and easily guarded."

"Getting to and from it…"

"I'll wear a suit," Chavri said. "It's what I did before the *dupatta*, and now, when I go out on the *Aurora Three*." She took a deep breath and slowed down. "Look, I know. I'm delicate. My health is not guaranteed, even with all the precautions. But I can't actually imagine any safer place for me than in one of the suits I wear for space travel. Independent air source. The most advanced filtration system. Head-to-toe covering."

"It's one thing to wear a suit on one of the rare occasions we allowed you to go to space, but it's another to walk the corridors of the palace in one, like some sort of..."

"Sick person," Chavri said, exasperation coming through despite her best efforts. "Some sort of sick person, Mother. Which is what I am. The *dupatta* was great—it let the people see a person, a princess, and not something sealed off from the world. But it was also a lie. I am sick. I have been sick. I will be sick. The whole province took up the habit of wearing veils just because I am sick, just to make sure no one exhaled anything my bio-filters couldn't keep from me. They *know* I'm sick. I don't see how being seen in a full-body suit would change that. And I won't be kept from my work just for...*decorum's sake*."

Chavri couldn't keep the disgust from her voice. Her chin was up and out, and she was working hard to keep breathing steady. She was at war with herself again, trying to find the balance of pushing back hard enough but not so hard that her parents could dismiss her as irrational. She really wanted to scream, "It's not fair!" She had, when she was younger, until she realized that it never helped.

"I understand that I have responsibilities as the heir. I understand that image matters. I have done everything, *everything* you have ever asked of me. But the work I do is important, too. And the truth is...I won't ever produce another heir for Moarga. But I can do something else that will help our province. Please, don't keep that from me."

"Chavri," her mother began, but her father held up his hand, silencing her.

"She's right," he told her. "She has never been content just to be, and has always fought to contribute what she can. It is honorable, and very becoming of an heir of Moarga." There was genuine pride in his voice and Chavri could feel her face warm with the compliment.

"How do we know her suit won't fail?" her mother demanded. "We need to eliminate risks, keep her safe."

"Sulina," he said softly. "She can't *only* be safe. She also needs to live her life. Or else what are we keeping her safe for?"

Chavri had never adored her father more. But she also understood her mother's fears.

She uncrossed her arms and stepped toward the glass, putting her palm flat against it. After a moment, her mother stepped forward and placed her hand over Chavri's. Just like when Chavri was little. She could see her mother's eyes tear up, remembering. Chavri had to blink hard to keep her own from doing the same. It seemed she spent her life trying to touch people through barriers.

"I *am* scared," she said at last. "I don't want you to think I'm not. I just don't want to live scared, you know?"

Her mother nodded. Her father smiled, and put his own hand against the glass, and Chavri mirrored his movement with her free hand. The three stood like that for a long moment. Chavri was the first to move away.

"You wanted to talk to me now for a reason, right? Are you leaving?"

"We're going to Mehmtok," her father said. "The delegation

stated that they are not sure it is as safe here as it could be. We'll have to continue our negotiations there. It took a lot to even get them here in the first place." He sighed. "This deal is too delicate not to go, even though we don't want to."

"When?"

"Tomorrow. You'll be back in your regular chambers tonight."

"No more wait-and-see?"

"The doctors have found nothing. I don't see any reason to keep you in this bubble."

Chavri tried not to sigh in relief. It had been a long few days under constant observation. Still, part of her was upset her parents were leaving, the small part of her who still had nightmares. She pushed that part away.

"And I can go back to work tomorrow?"

Her mother and father exchanged a look she couldn't read. It was one of those private couple's looks that no one on the outside could ever hope to translate, but which the couple in question always understood perfectly. It ended with her mother looking away, and blinking her eyes as if to clear some emotion from them.

"You can go back to work tomorrow," King Ardan told Chavri. "We'll say our goodbyes now. Your mother and I will leave before dawn."

Chavri nodded.

"Safe travels. May the gods hold you."

"May the gods hold you," her father replied.

"We love you," her mother said, looking deep into Chavri's eyes. "Stay safe."

Chapter 4

It was with practiced ease that Chavri programmed the mechanical arms in her chambers to help her put on her space suit. The suit was dark blue and black, fitted in the waist, but baggy in the legs and arms, insulation making it thick and somewhat stiff, like a winter coat. The robotic arms assisted Chavri as she pulled it up and over her legs, wrestling her hands down stiff sleeves, and wriggled the back up over her shoulders. The arms secured the back of her suit, and in the next motion, pulled a helmet down over her head. The mask of the helmet was perfectly clear and had a unique shape, flatter in the back where it was solid and the inside housed an onboard computer system and integrated communications. But the front curved out away from Chavri's face, leaving room for a headpiece that slid over her ears and had a microphone attached to the end of a small arm positioned to the right of Chavri's mouth. When she was wearing her suit on the planet, an external speaker and microphone allowed her to communicate with others, whether or not they wore communication devices.

The mechanical arms held out two gloves, one on either side of Chavri, and she shoved her hands in. With a twist, each glove was locked into her suit, while another twist sealed her helmet. Chavri heard a hiss, the sound of air being pumped into her newly airtight environment, and relaxed. The feeling of suffocating was still fresh in her mind, and she checked her oxygen tank and all her gauges to make sure everything was in working order.

Riska had personally overseen the inspection of her suit, and its decontamination process, and the tests done on it in the hermetically sealed room to ensure it functioned well and had no chance of accidental exposure. While she always had taken his presence for granted, over the last few days Riska had become Chavri's shadow. At some other time she might have been annoyed. But just then she felt grateful, and safer for his diligence.

Chavri completed the last of her safety checks and then made her way to the first of the double doors of her chambers. Her doors functioned much like the airlock on the *Aurora Three*, the official space ship for the royal family. It was the third ship the Moargan owned, and likely the last one, thanks to the metal shortage.

Stacia had said she had news, but wouldn't say what it was—just that Chavri would be excited. Chavri tried not to be annoyed with the lack of information. She hadn't seen Stacia since being allowed to return to her own chambers, and while she hadn't made any plans with her, Chavri somehow still thought Stacia might stop by. It would be different visiting with Stacia without her *dupatta*, since she would have to stay behind a force field, but at least they could have talked, really talked, without any sort of observation.

It made Chavri more anxious about going to the lab. The lab wasn't exactly a private space, and for some reason, she really wanted to see Stacia in private. She wasn't even sure what she wanted to say. Chavri shrugged the feeling off—she was just feeling lonely, she was sure. *Nothing I'm not used to*, she thought.

The inner door of Chavri's room opened, and Chavri waited

for fresh air to be pumped into the space between the doors, and for the second one to open as well, impatience making the time go slower.

Chavri used the time to daydream about what Stacia's news could be. Maybe the scans discovered the lost *Aurora One*. Her captain Madeline "Mad" Ordonez was a particular hero of Chavri's. Captain Ordonez pioneered space exploration on L'Mondeau, and the *Aurora One* was the largest and most advanced research vessel of the time. In fact, thanks to the metal shortage, it was still the largest vessel ever created from the crashed colony ship. Finding the ship would not only finally solve the mystery of what happened to her and her crew, it would allow Chavri and her team a better chance to continue the space program. With updated sensors and panels, the *Aurora One* could potentially find a real source of metal, or even find a way to send a message to the other colonies in the Interplanetary Alliance.

At last the door opened and Chavri was able to leave her chambers. Riska was standing outside in his usual spot, and he greeted her with his usual nod of recognition.

"You can probably guess my destination," she told him.

"You are very predictable," he said while he took his place behind her and to the left.

"Only out of necessity," she responded, her impatience making her annoyed. She imagined Riska sighing at her, but had never seen him do it and had to suppress the urge to turn and look.

At the end of the hall another door opened. Lysa, her second oldest attendant and ship pilot, stood guard in a grey veil uniform to Riska's. Lysa's dark green eyes expressed the smile her veil covered. Chavri kept her pace steady as Lysa joined in, taking the spot to Chavri's right and slightly forward of her. If Chavri reached out both arms, one toward each attendant, she wouldn't be able to touch either of them by a good two-hands-length. This was *dupatta* distance, and even with her fully suited, they fell into their usual walking pattern.

"You don't have to be veiled," she said to Lysa. *Or walk so far away*, she said only to herself.

"Try telling Riska that," Lysa countered.

"You may yet get your *dupatta* back," Riska said. "In time. I don't believe one malfunction in almost ten years warrants abandoning them completely."

Malfunction, Chavri thought. *Sure.*

"Though, obviously your mother didn't agree," Lysa added. Chavri grinned inside her helmet, her soft-booted feet feeling heavy and awkward on the carpeted hallway of the palace. She'd change into heavier boots once on the *Aurora Three*.

"I have to say, I'm fine with not wearing my *dupatta* today," she said.

"I bet," Lysa said, keeping her eyes forward. Her voice had a lot of sympathy in it though and Chavri was glad that neither of her attendants could see her face. She was sure her sudden sadness would be plain to see.

Chavri's hand-held beeped, and Chavri pulled it from her pocket without looking since her helmet limited her head movement. She held it up to eye level without changing her stride. This was a familiar, wide, and clear hallway, and her feet knew it better than her eyes anyway.

"Good news?" Lysa asked, keeping her eyes forward.

"Apparently," Chavri said, allowing herself a small smile. "Very good news. Stacia won't say what though until I get there."

"She is very much like her mother," Riska said. "Eva always loved her mysteries, too."

He didn't normally talk about his sister, and Chavri imagined that her most recent brush with death may have put him in mind of her last one, the same way it did her. She felt a huge twinge of guilt whenever Stacia's mother came up. Stacia was only a few weeks older than Chavri was, and thanks to Chavri, had spent almost her entire life without her mother. Chavri had tried apologizing for it when she was younger, but Stacia had told her it wasn't her fault, it was The Thirteenth's.

Still, Chavri wondered how Stacia managed to not hold any grudges against her.

Soon the trio was at the lab, and Chavri worked hard to keep her body still while waiting for the doors to open.

The door to the lab opened with a metallic groan, and Stacia came bounding forward, rushing to Chavri and pulling her into as tight a hug as her suit would allow. It was tight enough for Chavri to feel it, and she closed her eyes and imagined she could feel the warmth of Stacia's body, and not just the pressure of her hug. But the suit protected her even from that.

"That's one advantage of not being in a *dupatta*," Stacia said, pulling back enough to grin at Chavri.

"A very good one," Chavri said, smiling back, relieved by Stacia's warmth. "Now will you please tell me what you've been very carefully not telling me since the incident?"

"Remember those scans that were super promising and then not promising at all?"

Stacia lead Chavri into the middle of the room and began to type away at the center console. "They are actually the most promising scans we've had yet," Stacia said, her hands dancing along the type pad with practiced ease. She looked up as her movements created a projected image between her and Chavri. Chavri's eyes looked past her helmet edge to take in the information, scanning rapidly and seeing the final piece of Stacia's puzzle.

"The Kuntak Asteroid Belt," Chavri said. "You said it was a false positive."

"Did I?" Stacia said. "I guess I read the scans wrong. Anyway, I triple confirmed them this time, and there is definitely something there."

"But we can't tell what the something is from here," Chavri said. She glanced over at Lysa and Riska, each positioned on either side of the main door into the science lab.

"Not from here, no," Stacia confirmed.

Chavri could tell by his posture that Riska was definitely paying close attention to this exchange, even if he gave no indication he was.

"So we have to go out to see what it is," she said.

"Like we've done over a dozen times before," Stacia said.

"Sure," Chavri said. "Before."

"It's at least two days there, and another two back, so a minimum four days in space," Stacia noted.

"I suppose we don't both have to go," Chavri said, her tone clearly and intentionally disappointed by the prospect.

Stacia shook her head, but carefully.

"You are way better at interpreting those scans than I am. And I don't know what other team I could work with, or want to. If you don't go, I won't go."

Riska made a slight noise, as though he was delicately clearing his throat.

Chavri turned toward him.

"I know. I know everything you are going to say. And I have counters to all of it."

"Your parents," he began anyway.

"Are not here," Chavri said, interrupting. "And I'll be suited up the entire time and in the one place that The Thirteenth could never even think about getting to me. I'm pretty sure it's against their religion or something."

"The Thirteenth aren't the only things that can kill you," Riska said wryly.

"The increased risk of accident will be mitigated by the decreased risk of exposure. I think it's a fair trade." Chavri stood tall in front of him, a head taller than Stacia, but still much shorter than the older man. Lysa shifted slightly in her stance, the only betrayal of her own tense feelings in the moment. Riska was her supervisor—she couldn't weigh in, even if she wanted to.

"What happened with my *dupatta* shouldn't change things. My parents let me come back to work. Going up in the *Aurora Three* is part of my job. I want to do my job."

Once again Riska did not sigh. But the absence of the sigh was profoundly felt, and something in his shoulders suggested that he really wanted to.

"The lectures will be epic," he said, no particular feeling in his voice.

"We'll get through them, somehow," Chavri responded, and was rewarded with the slightest movement of Riska's left eyebrow, while Lysa's were shaped in a way that indicated a large grin under her veil. Stacia's own joy was very plain for anyone to see, but Chavri kept her expression as contained as she could.

"Register the flight path," Riska said to Stacia. "Pack her things and clear a route to the ship, extra security," he instructed Lysa. He turned to Chavri. "And you, young lady: I hope you know what you're doing."

Chapter 5

"I can't believe this is actually happening," Stacia said, her eyes scanning down a check list displayed on her hand-held.

"I can't believe Riska was so easily convinced," Chavri said.

"I honestly think he decided you might be safer in space. They're still investigating, you know. And at least in space no one can actually get to you."

The thought had occurred to Chavri as well.

"If my parents were here though, they'd throw up all sorts of blocks. Well, at least my mother would. As it is, they won't even get the message that we left until they get to Mehmtok. I may end up losing my space privileges for a long time after this."

"Not if we find something. Discovery has a way of easing disappointment."

Chavri took a deep breath and hoped that was true. Still, she'd be back before her parents would be, and hopefully by then, they would have gotten over their anger.

And either way, she was going to go to space. The excitement she had been afraid to feel earlier bubbled up inside her.

"Best. Timing. Ever," she said, grinning at Stacia.

Stacia grinned back.

"Yeah, I made sure of that."

"You didn't?"

"Didn't withhold information about the scans until your parents were out of town? Um. Yes. Of course I did. Otherwise they might have sent some other team or me without you. I knew that we'd convince Riska."

"Only because he hates saying no to you even more than he hates saying no to me," Chavri said, frowning slightly. She walked to the far wall and programmed the mechanical hands there to help Stacia into her suit. "You can't get in trouble for this, can you?"

"The results were easy enough to fake," Stacia said, stepping into her suit and letting the machine help her pull it up and over her hips. "Marcus was on the last few days, and you know he's not as thorough as Miranda. And just imagine what would have happened if I did let him see them? The real scans, I mean."

"He'd insist on going."

"And he'd do the laziest job possible, and even if these were what we hope they are, he'd probably miss the source anyway. And we'd be right back where we started with one more location 'checked off' that might actually have been a real lead." She shoved her hands into her gloves.

Chavri kept frowning as she grabbed Stacia's helmet off the wall.

"But you didn't tell me until today," she said, her back to Stacia.

"So you wouldn't be complicit, just in case I did get caught," Stacia countered. Chavri could hear her walking toward her but refused to turn around.

"Obviously I wanted to tell you right away," Stacia said. She grabbed Chavri's arm and turned her to force the taller girl to look at her. "I just wanted to make sure we could do this together. I don't want to go anywhere without you."

Chavri covered Stacia's hand with her own, something she could only do when completely suited up like this, and resisted the urge to pull her into another hug.

"You're not hiding anything else from me, are you?"

Stacia stood up on her tip-toes to press her forehead against the outside of Chavri's helmet.

"Never, my princess."

Chavri shoved Stacia away while trying unsuccessfully to suppress a grin.

"I hate when you call me that."

"I know," Stacia said, winking. "Now help me on with my helmet so that we can get going."

"You don't have to wear one the entire time," Chavri said, doing what she was told anyway.

"I'm just trying to get as good at moving around in these things as you are. I swear, if anyone was built for space travel, it's you."

Chavri felt herself blush at the compliment, even while part of her brain rejected it. She was only good at moving around in suits because she had been wearing one kind or another almost her entire life. Chavri finished securing Stacia's helmet, and pressed the button that would turn on Stacia's independent oxygen system. Stacia lightly tapped her helmet against Chavri's as a thank you.

Standing close together in a way only possible when Chavri was suited up, she and Stacia waited while forced air rushed over them, filling the airlock with the manufactured air that would be found in the space ship. This precaution was not for Chavri's benefit, but to ensure that no particles from L'Mondeau travelled with them into space. Fungus and bacteria had a way of growing in the most unusual places and could cause havoc in electrical systems. The electrical fire that took out the crew of the *Aurora Two* was the result of a rare fungus growing unseen inside a panel after water droplets had floated into it. It was the kind of trage-dy that the people of L'Mondeau wanted to be sure would only happen once.

Finally, the door to the *Aurora Three* opened, and Chavri was able to step inside. Immediately she felt the way she always did, that some part of her had come home.

Chapter 6

The *Aurora Three* was roughly wedge-shaped, with a narrower nose and wider rear end. The bridge was in the front and divided into two sections, a bank of consoles bisecting the first third of it, one pilot and operations seat on each side. Two more seats in the back each faced panels tied into the various sensor arrays. After the bridge was a cramped crew section with four cabins that were just big enough for a single person to slide into feet first. Their mess hall, such as it was, was after that, all their food and water stored in one place. Chavri subsisted on liquid meals while in space, since she could only take off her helmet in one of the airlocks and tried to do so as little as possible. Past the crew area was the heart of the ship, a much larger open space between two airlocks on either side that lead toward the main engineering section. It was also where they stored fuel, oxygen, and everything else they would need to keep the ship flying.

The *Aurora Three* wasn't pretty, per se, but it was functional.

It was quick work to get the ship ready for the pre-flight sequence, and during that time Lysa joined them. Riska stayed back in the control room where he could monitor their progress and be an intimidating presence to remind the operators there that the well-being of the nation's princess and only heir was in their hands. It was his usual post when Chavri went to space. Chavri asked once and was assured that even in the control room Riska didn't take off his veil. Chavri smiled at the thought.

Still, she was glad that Lysa didn't have such ideals, as her veil didn't really go with the rest of the space suit she was wearing. Chavri of course wouldn't be allowed to breathe the same air as the rest of the crew, and would keep her suit on for the entire flight. She didn't mind though. It would have been impossible in the small space to keep the kind of distance between her and the others that had to be maintained when she wore her special *dupatta*, even if she were still allowed to wear it. Plus, the view through the front of her helmet was much clearer than through the cloth. Of course, there was the added bonus of being able to casually bump into others and feel the impact of their bodies against hers. Lysa teased her about being clumsy, but no one actually minded when Chavri seemed to accidentally collide with them. The crew of the *Aurora Three* knew better than most how hard it was on Chavri to live constantly behind barriers.

Finally, the ship was ready for the pre-flight sequence, a series of checks that would ensure that everything was in proper order.

"Moarga Space Command to *Aurora Three*: get ready for final countdown. Over," said a familiar voice. Stacia grinned at Chavri. Riska wasn't usually the one to send them off, but Chavri was glad to hear his voice.

"MSC, this is *Aurora Three*, standing by for countdown," Lysa responded. "For the record, I am not wearing a veil. Over." Lysa's black hair was buzzed close to her head, a choice many guards made, and without her veil it could be clearly seen.

"*Aurora Three*, please look forward to a write-up when you get back planet-side. Over."

Chavri laughed.

"MSC, this is the princess of Moarga talking. Veils have been outlawed on *Aurora Three* by my order. Over."

"Princess Chavri, I don't believe you have the authority to do that. But I will make note of that in my report. Over."

"Are we counting down or not?" Stacia interjected. "Over," she added as an after-thought.

"We are indeed. Clamps disengaged. *Aurora Three*, countdown to take off in ten, nine, eight...."

Chavri pulled her restraints tighter against her suit. This part was always rough.

"...five, four, three, two, one."

The last clamp holding the *Aurora Three* let go with a groan, and the ship began to move rapidly down a large ramp that would launch it into the sky just as its rocket ignited.

It went as smoothly as possible, and then they were airborne. For a moment, everything depended on the rocket lighting up. Without it the *Aurora Three* wouldn't continue its upward climb. If it ignited too late, they wouldn't get enough momentum before hitting the atmosphere. If it went too early, they'd burn through too much fuel before breaking through. The timing had to be perfect.

A giant explosion caused the craft to surge up, and Chavri breathed a sigh of relief.

"MSC to *Aurora Three*, that was perfectly timed. My compliments to your pilot. Over."

Lysa grinned.

"Be sure to include that in your report as well," she said. "Over."

"Will do," Riska said. "May the gods hold you, *Aurora Three*.

Over."

"May the gods hold you," Chavri said. "*Aurora Three* going offline for atmospheric break. *Aurora Three*, over and out."

Chavri felt the familiar thrill as the force of their flight threw her back against her seat, her head rattling thanks to the vibration of the ship. She was able to turn enough to make eye contact with Stacia, and both of them were grinning wide.

At last, the *Aurora Three* broke through the atmosphere, Lysa guiding the ship away from the blue-green planet below them. Chavri craned her head the other way to look out a small window and onto a shrinking view of L'Mondeau. She felt the breath catch in her chest. She always felt her breath catch in her chest at that view.

"Laying in a course for the Kuntak Asteroid Belt," Lysa announced.

"Laying in a course to destiny!" Stacia amended. Chavri and Lysa both laughed at her.

"No pressure," Chavri said.

"I really feel like this trip is the one," Stacia said. Chavri didn't fully share her optimism. Probably they would just get to the belt, do more up close scans, and find some trace metal that was too small to even bother trying to mine. Or maybe it was a false positive. Or maybe something else that also meant this wasn't the answer they'd been looking for. It was definitely probably not the *Aurora One*, whose last contact with Moarga was from a position a half-a-day's travel in the opposite direction from the Kuntak. Chavri wanted to keep her expectations low.

"You don't seem as excited as I am," Stacia said, tapping

Chavri's helmet to get her attention.

"I guess I'm still feeling rattled, still looking for the ways things can go wrong."

"That's not a bad thing," Lysa chimed in. "Caution is always prudent."

"Things won't go wrong." Stacia looked determined. "I have a good feeling about this trip."

"You always have a good feeling about every trip," Chavri said.

"Well this is an extra special good feeling. The Kuntak isn't well explored. I just know we'll find something!"

Chavri hoped Stacia was right. Or rather, she hoped that the something that Stacia knew they would find would be good.

Chavri stared out the window at the shrinking shape of L'Mondeau below her and felt very glad to be far away from it. Her gaze moved out to look at the stars, and a familiar thrill overcame her—she was out among the stars, seeing things that almost no one else on L'Mondeau got to see. She felt both very special and very small.

It was her fifteenth time in space. But some things never got old.

PART III:

The Spindle

Partly because she was too hasty, partly because she was a little heedless, but also because the fairy decree had ordained it, no sooner had she seized the spindle than she pricked her hand and fell down in a swoon.

Charles Perrault, The Sleeping Beauty in the Wood

Chapter 7

Chavri frowned at the readouts on the console in front of her.

"This doesn't look like what I was expecting," she said. Stacia peered around her shoulder, and Chavri could see her nod inside her helmet.

"I know. Me neither. Is it weird that's why I think it's so promising?"

"Yes, yes, it is."

Stacia stuck her tongue out at Chavri and wiggled it, showing off a small blue post in its center. Chavri laughed. Stacia didn't often show her piercing off since it was not something her uncle Riska approved of.

"We're coming up on the edge of the Kuntak," Lysa announced from the other side of the small flight deck of the ship. "I'm telling you now, mija," she said to Chavri. "I am not taking us in there."

"That's not the plan," she retorted.

"The field is unstable, and it's near impossible to predict the path of the asteroids in time to avoid them. And we don't have the kind of shielding necessary to survive any decent impact," Lysa said.

"We heard you the first time," Stacia said, clearly rolling her eyes even if Lysa couldn't see them.

"Riska made you promise not to travel there, didn't he?" Chavri asked. Lysa smiled.

"He's the boss," she said. "And you've had enough scares lately."

Secretly, Chavri agreed, though she didn't want Stacia to know that.

Stacia did not seem the least bit convinced that they shouldn't go into the belt. She tried her best to indicate her displeasure as she made her way back over to her own console, but was unable to properly stomp in zero gravity and had to settle for making loud contact with her chair. Chavri might have laughed at her if she wasn't sure it would just piss her off more. Nerves among the crew over the past two days had been frayed, to say the least. The closer they got to the Kuntak, the more their various feelings of excitement, apprehension, and frustration collided. Tempers had been getting short.

Chavri checked her sensor readings again.

"I just don't get it. There is something in there, that's for sure. But the reading is just so...sporadic. Like maybe something is blocking the scan. Could it be something in the asteroids?"

"I'm trying to compensate for it, whatever it is. Because this close in what I'm actually reading doesn't make any sense."

"Right. Unless somehow these asteroids have purified aluminum in them, and not bauxite."

"Sure, with trace amounts of titanium, and even some ceramics."

"Hey, are you sure we aren't just bouncing the signal off the rocks and scanning our own ship?" Lysa asked. "Because that's all the things we have. Plus, the shielding."

"That would be horrible!" Stacia said, running another type

of scan to search for reflection of the signal.

"I don't think that's what's happening," Chavri said, and stared hard at her readout as though daring her eyes to see something else. She checked it again, a hunch building into a theory, her theory becoming more real with every reading she registered. "Uh, guys? I think I know why it seems like we're reading a space ship…"

She punched a few more buttons on her pad and then waited for the result to ping. Suddenly her theory wasn't just a theory anymore.

"Is that…?" Stacia pushed off from her console to crowd behind Chavri and look over her shoulder. Curiosity had Lysa craning her neck, though she didn't leave her post.

"The source of the metal you picked up from L'Mondeau? Yes, yes it is."

They both stared at the shape that their computer created out of the results from all the scans they had conducted.

"Impossible!" Stacia said. "I mean, how, just how?"

Chavri shook her head, but she had another theory that was starting to form.

The computer was displaying a space ship. And only one had ever gone missing in L'Mondeau space.

"We need to contact Moarga Space Command," Chavri said, excitement and fear combining to create a thread of sweat down her spine.

"We're two days out. Any signal we send will take thirty minutes to get there, and another thirty to get a reply," Lysa said. "Plus, interference from the asteroids is creating a lot of static.

We need to move away from the belt to contact MSC and wait for a reply."

"Give me a few more minutes to scan the area, see if I can get a better idea of the location of the ship," Chavri said.

"I don't like the level of interference I'm getting," Lysa said.

"We're perfectly safe. We'll get the scans and go." Stacia's annoyance seemed to be amplified by her excitement.

"I'll give you three minutes, then we move away," Lysa said. "So be quick. And thorough."

Neither Stacia nor Chavri replied, their hands flying over the pads as they programmed in instructions to the ship's computer. Chavri had no idea how the *Aurora One* ended up in the Kuntak, but as it had been lost for centuries, she supposed it could have drifted. From her scans, it didn't seem to have any structural integrity problems, no clear indication of what happened to it. It was powered down, either in sleep mode or out of juice. Chavri's mind raced with possibilities.

A loud clanging noise from Lysa's station pulled her and Stacia way from their pads.

"Status!" Chavri shouted.

"Primary propulsion systems offline!" Lysa yelled back. "I think there's a…"

An explosion in the aft sector of the ship rocked the three women hard, Lysa slamming her helmeted head into her console with an audible crack.

"Lysa!" Chavri shouted. She began to undo her restraints when Stacia yelled at her.

"No! Stay put! Report the readings." She scrambled out of

her seat instead, holding on to whatever she could as she made her way to Lysa.

"It came from the primary fuel lines on the starboard side," Chavri reported. "I'm shutting down all air flow to the area to see if that will keep the fire from spreading. How's Lysa?"

"Alive. And conscious, if barely." Stacia yanked Lysa's helmet off her head and revealed a large cut on Lysa's forehead. "She didn't have the motion stabilizers active."

Every helmet in their space suits created a reactive cushion of air around their heads in case of severe turbulence or other impact. This safety feature was part of the reason why the helmet was the size it was. Without it activated, Lysa's head banged around inside her helmet with almost no resistance.

"Neither do you," Chavri chided. She was forced to take all the safety precautions, staying strapped in when not moving about the cabin, keeping all her stabilizers active at all times, having multiple backs ups to her air tanks. But the other women had grown lazy about theirs.

Stacia stopped checking on Lysa long enough to twist her own helmet off her head.

"What if something happens to life support?" Chavri shouted.

"Keep working on the fire," Stacia yelled back. Technically, even though Chavri was the heir, on the *Aurora Three*, Stacia outranked her. Chavri pulled her attention away from her friends to focus on the readouts, programming the computer to take the necessary steps to put out the fire. If she didn't get it under control, it could destroy the ship, or at least make it uninhabitable.

She tracked the path of the fire, shutting down any systems that could be impacted.

"Stacia, lock down the bridge. I need to vent the air everywhere else."

"Roger." Stacia floated her way over to the main door, yanking it closed and cranking the wheel to seal it. She then hurried back to Lysa, stopping on the way to sweep up a first aid kit.

"Status!" she yelled out.

"Decompressing now." Chavri watched the meter readings carefully—they were venting a lot of air in this process, and the fire had already eaten up a great deal. Finally, the decompression cycle was complete and she checked the internal sensors. "Fire is out! How's Lysa?"

"Hanging in there," Chavri heard Lysa say, and tension drained from her shoulders. "What happened?"

"I'm not sure. There was a fire, and an explosion, and…it's all out now."

But the ship was still blaring alarms.

"Proximity alert," Lysa called out. "The explosion, the fire, the venting, it's knocked us off course. We're going into the Kuntak."

"Well, we should probably not do that, right?" Chavri said. Her readings were telling her the same thing. "Impact in two minutes."

"Primary propulsion is fried. I can't seem to switch to secondary from here."

"We'll have to do it manually," Stacia called, putting a bandage over Lysa's head. "How long to re-pressurize engineering?

I'll have to go in."

Chavri had already started the sequence. The issue wasn't air—their suits and helmets would provide that. The issue was that the pressure outside the bridge and inside the bridge didn't match, and that meant they wouldn't be able to get the door open, not without sucking all the air out of the bridge as well. That would mean losing even more air. And more importantly, Chavri wasn't sure that Lysa's helmet was up to the task.

"Forty-five seconds remaining."

"Shit," Stacia said. She grabbed her helmet and made her way to the door, putting it on as she went.

"Time till impact, one minute and fifteen seconds," Lysa called. "This is going to be ridiculously close."

"Stacia, stabilizers," Chavri said, and Stacia pushed the sequence into the pad attached to her wrist that turned them on.

The women waited while Chavri called out the count down until pressurization completed in fifteen second intervals: "Thirty seconds. Fifteen seconds." Finally, she was down to fives. "Ten. Five. Pressurization complete."

Chavri tried to follow Stacia's movements through the cameras placed throughout the ship. She watched as Stacia twisted the door lock and yanked the door open and shoved herself forward like a swimmer kicking off the back wall, speeding past crew quarters. Chavri had to turn her focus back to her readouts and hope Stacia would be okay. She had a moment of relief when she heard Stacia shouting over coms.

"Secondary propulsion online!" she said.

"Engaging thrusters," Lysa called back.

"Time to impact, fifteen seconds," Chavri added.

"We're going to hit," Lysa said. "Slowing our descent. Brace for impact."

Chavri could feel the thrusters engage, pushing her body one way. A few seconds later, she felt the impact of the *Aurora Three* against the asteroid, and her body flopped the other way. With the help of the thrusters, the ship ricocheted off, and again, her body was tossed the opposite direction.

"Damage report!"

"Damage to the starboard hull. Integrity holding. Stacia, make sure the starboard airlock is sealed."

"On it!" Stacia yelled. After a while, she came back on coms. "Airlock secure. Ladies, reentry is going to be a bitch."

Chavri checked her sensors and the cameras. There was a hole where the starboard airlock used to be. Reentry was definitely going to be a bitch.

Chavri stayed focused on her readouts, frustrated by what she was seeing. The *Aurora Three* had taken heavy damage. She looked out the window and saw parts of her ship floating by in space. Maybe they could try to retrieve them, but by the time they got themselves stabilized and on their way, the metal would likely be gone.

"Secondary propulsion still online," Lysa called. "I'm trying to stabilize her. We are fully in the field, I repeat, we are fully in the field."

Stacia came back into the bridge, made her way to her station and took the time to strap herself in.

"We're going to keep getting banged around unless we find

something big enough to attach to."

"Sending you a destination now," Chavri said.

"That takes us further in," Lysa said.

"Yeah, but it's the only place I can find that could keep us remotely safe."

"And how do we get back out?" Stacia asked.

"We'll figure that out after we assess the damage, and make what repairs can be made. Chavri's right—we have to go further in. We'll take too many hits trying to get out in this condition." Lysa shook her head as she plugged in their new destination. "Your uncle's going to kill me."

"We have to get back to him first," Stacia said. "Chavri, you seeing this?"

Chavri knew exactly what Stacia was talking about, and not only had she seen it, she planned it. The asteroid they were maneuvering toward did in fact match their need, but that's not why she picked it. It took several more minutes of travel, but as the *Aurora Three* swung into view of the dark side of the asteroid, something else came into view with it.

"Gods," Lysa said. "It's bigger than I thought."

Chavri stared out the window, her eyes confirming what her readouts had already told her: they were headed directly toward the *Aurora One*.

Chapter 8

Chavri finished her inspection of the burned-out conduit and leaned back against the opposite bulkhead.

"Sabotage," she said. "There's no other explanation."

"But how? This ship is one of the most heavily guarded in the province. In any province. Not to mention the fact that The Thirteenth abhors technology. How would they even know how to do this?" Stacia shook her head and checked her hand-held again.

"Who did you tell about the scans?" Lysa asked. Her head was still wrapped, and her left wrist as well, a sprain that wasn't really felt until the immediate danger was over. Stacia had a few bruises, but Chavri remained injury free.

"No one. Just Chavri."

"And then she told me they were a false positive. And then she told me they were actually a real positive. But the last two were in person."

"But the first time was via hand-held?" Lysa frowned.

"You think I was hacked?" Chavri had to work to keep her breathing steady. She didn't want her growing alarm to panic either of the other two.

"It's a possibility."

"Or me," Stacia said. "I'd probably be an easier target. But still, all the rest."

"It actually gives credence to a theory that Riska had, and the real reason why he let us take this trip."

Chavri closed her eyes, as though that might protect her from the truth. "He thought we would be safer up here. Someone inside the palace is working with The Thirteenth."

"How?" Stacia asked. "Why? I mean…I just don't…"

Chavri felt the same way. She didn't want to accept the truth of it any more than Stacia did. But it seemed that The Thirteenth weren't above using technology to win the war against technology.

"The good news is that the list of people who might be capable of setting something like this up—a delayed accident—is very small." Lysa didn't seem pleased by her good news.

"Sure, so if we ever get back to Moarga, we'll have a list of suspects." Chavri turned away from the others and pulled herself toward the door out of engineering. This was her fault. The Thirteenth were trying to kill her, again. And this meant that her *dupatta* wasn't just a random malfunction. Gods, it probably meant that none of the tech in her life, tech she needed to stay alive, could be trusted.

She'd never wanted to rip her helmet off more. Her breathing was speeding up, and a warning system in her suit started to chime—breathing like this was using up too much air. Part of her knew better, knew she needed to use one of her calming exercises. The other part of her was glad she was using up air, glad she was triggering alarms in the suit. She imagined the sound meant the suit was angry at her, and that helped fuel her anger. She wanted to make noise, too. She wanted to yell, scream, or punch something.

But more than anything, she wanted out. Out of the suit, out of the ship, out of her life.

"Chavri." She felt Lysa's hand on her shoulder, pulling her around.

"Don't," Chavri said, trying to back away. But the older woman was much stronger, and the truth was she didn't try that hard. Lysa pulled Chavri into a hug, resting her bandaged head on the outside of Chavri's helmet.

"This isn't your fault."

Chavri felt hot tears roll down her face, and wished she could wipe them away. If she didn't stop crying soon, her nose was going to start to run, and she didn't really have a way to deal with that, either. Not without going into the airlock, alone, as she did whenever she needed a break from her helmet. She wasn't sure she trusted herself to be alone right then. Besides, they couldn't waste air clearing and filling the airlock again.

"I'm fine," she said, taking slow breaths and focusing on lowering her heart rate. "Really."

"I know," Lysa said. "Though it would also be fine if you weren't." She squeezed Chavri one more time and then let her go, causing Chavri to float back a little until she braced herself on one of the many handles throughout the ship. Chavri gave her a smile to prove that she really was managing, but the smile Lysa returned looked very sad.

"We'll worry about The Thirteenth when we get out of here," Stacia said, floating up behind Lysa.

"Yeah," Lysa agreed. "So, let's get this over with. Damage report."

"Primary propulsion is gone. We have damage all along the starboard side, including the airlock. We lost sixty percent of our air and forty percent of our fuel. And if we don't find a way to repair the starboard shielding, there's a strong chance that we'll burn up on reentry." Stacia looked appropriately glum.

"But," Chavri said, "back up propulsion is enough to get us back to L'Mondeau, even with our fuel supply low. And we have a second ship to raid for parts, maybe even air."

Stacia looked at Lysa, and Lysa sighed.

"I know that's why you put us here, but I don't like it. We have no idea what happened to the *Aurora One*, or her crew. The only thing we know is that she has been missing for, what, almost two hundred years? I mean, what would still be working?"

"A lot, potentially," Chavri said. "From what the scans say, she has full hull integrity, and I can't find anything wrong with her systems. No life signs, but that's to be expected. Space has a way of preserving things. I can't be sure, but I think I even found air tanks on her. We need air."

"We don't," Lysa said. "Or rather, you don't. Your supply was untouched. You have more than enough to get back to L'Mondeau."

"It's not enough for all three of us," Chavri said. "Even if your helmet wasn't cracked."

"That's not what she's saying," Stacia said.

"Oh, I know what's she's saying, and I'm telling you, no. We're not pulling that 'you're the heir' shit. We're not. We're all going back or none of us are."

Lysa and Stacia exchanged a look and Chavri had to turn away again before she lost her temper, closing her eyes tightly against the tears she wanted to cry.

"Please. We're in this together. Let's be in this together. I don't want to go back without you." She meant both of them, of course. But she meant Stacia more. She literally could not imagine living in a world without Stacia in it.

Stacia reached out and squeezed Chavri's right shoulder, and after a minute, Lysa squeezed her left. Chavri opened her eyes and looked at them both.

"Whatever you say, my princess," Stacia said. Chavri laughed, but instead of pushing her away, she grabbed Stacia and hugged her tightly, keeping hold of Lysa at the same time. Lysa wrapped her arms around the two younger women, and they stayed like that for a long moment, unanchored, and slowly turning.

"All right," she said at last, pulling away. "Stacia, get ready for your first ever away mission. You're going to the *Aurora One*."

Chapter 9

Chavri monitored her chronometer closely, watching as each second ticked by. Stacia had been out of contact for almost two entire minutes, and it was all Chavri could do to not yell out her name just to get a reply. There had been no way to properly line up the ships so that their airlocks met, and Stacia had to push herself off the *Aurora Three*'s airlock and float to *Aurora One*'s. During transit, Stacia discovered that something in the asteroid they were sheltering by caused radio interference. Lysa was able to work around it, but only in timed sporadic bursts. It was taking a lot of energy to break through the interference, and they didn't have enough to spare for more than that. It was quickly decided that they would communicate in thirty-second bursts every two minutes. Chavri hated that plan.

Finally, static on the coms line signaled Stacia was about to speak.

"I'm in what looks like the mess hall," she said. "This ship is a lot bigger than ours. I know it had a crew of ten, but it could easily house twice that."

The idea of a ship that could hold twenty crew members was nearly unbelievable to Chavri. She knew from reading about it that the *Aurora One* was the biggest of its time, but the largest ship currently operating was in Mehmtok. That ship could only hold up to a dozen people if they really liked each other, and eight if they wanted a normal amount of space.

"Any sign of…anything?" Chavri asked.

"You mean like bodies? None, yet."

Chavri shivered. As much as she would have liked to have been the one to explore the *Aurora One*, she was glad that she wouldn't have to see any corpses.

Stacia's initial scans had confirmed that the *Aurora One* had no structural damage. But so far, it didn't seem to have a crew, either.

"Heading to main engineering. If that matches the size of the rest of this ship, I'm expecting to be impressed."

"Heading into another blackout cycle in ten seconds," Lysa said.

"That was too fast," Chavri complained.

"You think your side is bad. Trust me, mine is worse," Stacia said. "Talk to you again in…."

But the signal cut out. Chavri reset her timer, counting down until the next communication.

"I hate this," she said.

"Me too," Lysa said. "I feel like I should have gone."

"With a head injury and busted helmet?"

"We should have packed a spare. Why didn't we pack a spare?"

"Because no one imagined we'd be taking a spacewalk," Chavri said. "Besides, if you'd left, then you wouldn't be able to guard me. What does your protocol say?"

Chavri already knew the answer but wanted to make Lysa say it.

"That I stay with you at all times, no matter what."

"So it was always going to be Stacia."

Chavri fiddled with the buckles that were keeping her anchored to her chair.

"And you're the pilot," she added.

"You could fly us home if you needed to," Lysa said.

They both turned to stare at the chronometer.

"I really hate this," Chavri said. Lysa patted her hand.

"She's fine. You'll see."

But the knot in Chavri's stomach thought otherwise. The seconds ticked by, and at last the two minute window was up.

The coms unit automatically clicked on, and static greeted them.

"Status update?" Lysa asked. After a moment, she checked the com's channel to make sure it was active. "Stacia? Are you there? Please respond, over."

Chavri could feel panic rising in her throat like bile. Her eyes watched as the seconds of their tiny window of communication slipped away.

"Stacia?"

"Ten seconds left," Lysa announced. "Stacia, please respond!"

"Stacia!"

But the seconds counted down and the static clicked off.

"Shit," Lysa said.

Chavri undid her restraints and pushed herself off her chair.

"What are you doing?" Lysa asked.

"Going after her."

"No, you're not!" The older woman anchored herself on a chair and then pulled Chavri back toward her. "We don't know what happened. We don't even know if she is in trouble. And even if she is, you cannot be the person to go over there."

"There's no one else," Chavri said. "Your helmet is busted, and I can't give you mine. Maybe if the other airlock was still here, and you left me in there and took my helmet. Or maybe if we had more than tape to cover the crack in the helmet. Or maybe if any number of things were different, I wouldn't be the one who had to go to the *Aurora One*. But this is where we are, and this is what will have to happen."

"Wait. Give it another cycle. If we don't hear from her on the next loop…."

"You'll let me go?"

Lysa sighed. It was clear that the last thing she wanted was to say yes, but after a moment she nodded anyway.

"I'll let you go."

Chavri pulled herself back into her chair, looping one of the straps loosely over her arm as she and Lysa stared at the chronometer again.

Finally, static.

"Stacia!" Chavri yelled into her head piece. But she only got silence back.

"Stacia, you need to reply!" Lysa's voice had an edge to it that Chavri had never heard before. She had never heard her attendant sound panicked. She decided she really didn't like the sound.

"Stacia, if you don't reply, I'm coming to get you."

But only static greeted them. Chavri tried to listen through the static, see if she could at least hear Stacia breathing. It was too much to ask of the com system, she knew, but she still tried.

Then the static wasn't there anymore either.

"End of the loop," Lysa said.

Chavri untangled her arm and pushed off again, heading for the airlock.

"Wait!" Lysa called after her. Chavri ignored her and started the sequence to re-pressurize the airlock so that she could go into it.

"We're going to have the same communication issues. What do I do if I don't hear from you?"

"You get the *Aurora Three* back to open space and call for help. If you think you can make it, you head back to L'Mondeau."

"Then that's what we should be doing now. It's what we should have done before trying to go to *Aurora One*."

She put her hand on Chavri's shoulder to try to get her attention, and Chavri shrugged it off.

"And if Stacia was still with us, I'd be down with that plan. But since she's not, I'm going after her."

"So that you'll get lost too?"

"Look," Chavri said, finally turning to face her attendant. "When Stacia set out, we didn't know about the communications issues. Now we do. We didn't know about the interior of the ship. Now, thanks to the readings she sent back, we do. You'll give me a half hour. Forty-five minutes if you're feeling generous. And if you don't hear from either of us or I don't come back, you go get help."

"This is insane," Lysa said, shaking her head. "I cannot let you do this. I just can't. No way."

"And I can't leave her there. I can't. I just…I can't."

Chavri felt the sobs building in her chest and had to take a second to close her eyes and force them back down. Getting hysterical wasn't going to save Stacia. Once she felt calm enough, she opened her eyes again.

Both of them jumped at the sound of static.

"Another loop is starting," Lysa said. For the next thirty seconds they stood still, hardly breathing, trying to hear whatever could be heard in the static while the airlock finished pressurizing. The static stopped giving them no new information.

Chavri looked into Lysa's eyes and saw the tears in them she dared not shed. Lysa put her hand out, and Chavri took it.

"Thirty minutes," she said. "Bring her back. Bring yourself back."

"May the gods hold you," Chavri said.

"May the gods hold you," Lysa responded. Then she let go of Chavri's hand and helped her with the door to the airlock.

Another com loop passed while Chavri waited for the airlock to depressurize, and another one as she made her way to the *Aurora One*'s airlock— lead to a closed door a terrifying trip where she floated completely unmoored in space until momentum banged her up against the other ship. Fortunately, Stacia had closed the inner door. Unfortunately, she hadn't depressurized the airlock, assuming she would be the next person in it, and Chavri had to hold on tight as the force of air being sucked out of the open airlock knocked her back. It took all her strength to stop herself from being flung away like a ragdoll.

Once her heart stopped pounding in her ears, she carefully made her way into the airlock, struggling slightly to pull the door closed behind her. The controls inside the *Aurora One* were very similar to the ones on the *Aurora Three*, and it was easy enough to figure out how to pressurize the airlock.

She heard static on her radio while she was waiting.

"Chavri! Chavri, what was that?"

"Stacia had left the airlock pressurized. But the door is un-damaged, and so am I. Waiting for the all clear to open the inner door."

Chavri wanted to call out Stacia's name—they were using the same channel, just in case, but instead listened to the static with growing dread.

"The door is green," she told Lysa. "I'm going in." She looked down at her chronometer and saw that the thirty second window was almost up. "Stand by," she said.

And then, nothing. No sound. No static. Just her breath rasping loudly inside her suit. That had been the worst part, the silence.

Chavri entered a large open area that appeared to be used for storage. Space suits lined one wall, and she made a note to herself to try to snag one for Lysa. To her right was a main corridor, the light on her right wrist sweeping from side to side to take everything in. She turned the other direction to see if there was anything that way, but it led to a closed door. It was completely dark everywhere she didn't shine her light, and childhood fears gnawed up her spine and whispered in her ear. Her scans told her there was nothing around her, that she was alone. Safe. But the darkness told her that she was both too alone and not alone enough, her imagination filling the darkness with things that could evade her scans. She tried to picture what could have taken Stacia, what could still hurt her. Darkness wasn't safe, couldn't be safe, and she shouldn't turn her back on it.

Chavri focused on her breathing, her light, and on what was real. Double checking her wrist-pad to make sure she was following the same path Stacia transmitted, Chavri headed to the right, turning her back on the darkness. For Stacia, she told herself.

She came to a junction, with the choice to go up or down. The bridge should be up, based on the scans they were able to take and her understanding of the most logical layout for a ship. But Stacia had gone down, toward the mess hall, and toward where their scans said engineering was.

"Chavri, come in!" Lysa said through her headpiece. The sound of her voice was so sudden that Chavri had made a sound like a swallowed squeal in the back of her throat before registering what she was hearing. It took precious seconds for her to calm herself down and reply.

"Here," she said. "I'm here. I'm retracing her steps, heading toward engineering."

"That's where we lost her," Lysa said. She sounded as nervous as Chavri felt.

"Yep, but I'm a much more cautious person than she is," Chavri countered. Lysa chuckled weakly through her headpiece.

"Not cautious enough. Wasn't this trip your idea?"

"All Stacia's. She's the daring one."

"Ten seconds," Lysa chimed. It was amazing how fast the time went.

"I'll talk to you in two minutes," Chavri said, and really hoped that was true.

"Two minutes. Don't get lost on me."

Then, silence.

Chavri took a steady breath and kept her flashlight up as she moved down the hall toward where she thought Stacia had gone. She glanced down at her wrist-pad, scanning for any sign of Stacia. She was getting a reading of something, but it was hard to make out, and Chavri was more focused on actually seeing what was in front of her than reading about it on her pad.

In all her years of wearing suits, masks, and veils, Chavri had always had to fight the irrational desire to tear them off. She had always wanted to feel wind or rain on her face, or even just to see a loved one without any barrier between them.

This was the first time that Chavri felt absolutely certain she didn't want to take her helmet off. She mentally thanked whatever engineer designed it for the attention they gave to the viewing capacity of it. She could see very clearly what was in front of her, and a fair amount of her periphery as well, dimly lit up by a small light attached to her headpiece.

She did her best to keep the flashlight on her wrist steady, since movement in the light caused too many moving shadows, and moving shadows caused too many bad thoughts. Finally, she got to another junction, this one leading in only one other direction—down. After a moment's consideration, Chavri decided to go down head first so that she could see anything that was on the bottom of it. She pulled herself down the ladder with one hand, keeping the other up and her light out. When her head cleared the opening below her, she used the edge of the bulkhead to brace herself, carefully swinging her legs back down so that she was more or less upright, and surveying what was in front of her before moving on.

But what was in front of her didn't make any sense.

The door to engineering was open, and something was coming out of the door and into the hallway, and it took Chavri several heartbeats before she realized that it wasn't moving. She traced the shape of it with her light. It looked like a giant root system of some kind that was lining the ceiling and floor and preventing the door from closing. The root, tree-thick by the door, stretched down the hall toward Chavri, getting smaller and thinner, and the part closest to her looked like a tendril of hair. Chavri pushed gently off her position, floating easily over the root, and dragging her hand lightly against the wall to help slow her momentum. She didn't want to make it through the door without seeing what was on the other side. The roots around the door were so thick that there was no way to stop her momentum without touching them, something she felt sure she shouldn't do. She pulled a wrench from her belt and held it out in such a way that it caught the upper edge of the door, bouncing her back momentarily before she quickly switched it to the other side of the door lip and used it as an anchor to keep from floating away. She shone her light into engineering, her eyes searching and not fully able to take in what she was seeing.

What she thought were roots now looked more like vines, and they had wound themselves around everything in the large room. They were thickest toward the center, crowded around some object that Chavri couldn't see. She searched them, terrified at what she might find, until she caught a glimpse of a boot to her right. She used the wrench to push her body forward, then used to it to push free-floating vines out of her path until she got to the boot, hooking the wrench on a thick vine to help steady herself. The boot was attached to a leg, and the leg was attached to a body that had become tangled up in that same vine. With a slight pull, the body came free. Chavri had to steady herself again, as the effort caused her to float away. Finally, she was able to get the body turned around, pulling the head toward her.

She muffled her own scream and forced herself to be still as the figure spun around. It was then that she saw the head was male, and that he wasn't wearing a helmet. He was frozen stiff, which would be expected if he had been exposed to space, but didn't make any sense inside the *Aurora One*. There had been no hull breaches on any of the scans they were able to take, and there was still air in the ship or else the airlock wouldn't have needed to be pressurized. The frozen man seemed to be covered in something, a light dusting of something vaguely orangish that seemed particularly concentrated by his nose and mouth. Not sure what else to do with him, Chavri scanned his body with her pad and then pushed him gently away. He bumped into a nearby vine, twisting in air so that his stiff arm snagged it, and then was more or less still.

Chavri let out a breath she didn't know she had been holding, and looked down at her chronometer.

Shit. The com loop should have started up again, and she should have been hearing Lysa. Something in the room must have been blocking communication, and while Lysa had the power to break through a block on her end, Chavri's suit didn't. She could only hope once she got out of engineering, her coms would come back online.

She resumed her scan of the room with new urgency. Now that she was past the door and into the heart of engineering, she could see other bodies. The vines, such as they were, seemed mostly to grow on the floor and walls, growing out of a central system in the middle, and the bodies getting tangled in them seemed more accidental, as if the bodies had floated into the vines rather than the vines wrapping around the bodies. That was a small comfort, as Chavri kept waiting for one of the vines to snatch her up, like in a horror vid. Chavri kept scanning the room, mentally counting the bodies.

When she got to ten in her count, she searched for another with immense trepidation, not sure if she wanted to find one or not. There were ten members of the *Aurora One* crew, and at this point, they were all accounted for. Any additional body would have to be Stacia's.

Chavri slowly turned and swung her flashlight back by the door to the hallway, trying to see if she missed anything back that way.

And then she saw it—a hand, dangling down from above the door. Chavri pointed her light up and scanned the body quickly, noticing right away that the colors of the suit were different than the ones of the *Aurora One* crew, and still not wanting to believe what she was seeing. But the body lazily spun around, the face coming directly into Chavri's light, a light attached to the headpiece shining back at her.

Stacia. Her eyes were closed, and she didn't appear to be conscious. A quick inspection revealed nothing wrong with her helmet or suit, as far as Chavri could tell from that angle, and the flashlight on Stacia's wrist still on and pointing up in a way that Chavri wouldn't have seen the light when she came in. Stacia's wrist-pad seemed to still be on as well, still scanning. She just wasn't moving.

Chavri pushed off toward her, careful to anchor herself in the doorway before dragging Stacia's floating body back down toward her.

"Stacia!" she called out, hoping that maybe the com would kick in, maybe Stacia would hear her. "Stacia, please answer."

But she couldn't hear anything through her headpiece, not even static. And Stacia didn't move. Chavri knew there was something wrong with Stacia, something wrong with her suit maybe, but she also knew that if she stopped to look, or to really think about what was happening, she would shut down and never be able to move again. And she wanted more than anything to get out of that room, away from the strange vines and frozen people, and back to Lysa.

Lysa would be able to help Stacia. Lysa would know what to do.

Chavri pulled a retractable wire out from her belt and clipped the end of it onto Stacia's belt, making sure there was a fair amount of slack between them before locking the device so that it wouldn't coil the wire back into itself. Then she pulled herself through the doorway of engineering, checking the line to make sure that Stacia floated through the correct way and didn't snag on the edges. Chavri landed hard against the back wall, and wrapped her arm around the ladder to keep herself from bouncing away while bracing for the impact of Stacia's body against hers. She held it still and then gently pushed it up, keeping hold of the ladder, and propelled herself up after Stacia, yanking on the wire between them to make sure Stacia didn't hit her head at the top of the junction. It took some maneuvering to get through that with two floating bodies, and it took every zero-gravity physics lesson that Chavri ever had to do it successfully.

Every time doubt and fear and frustration threatened to overcome her, Chavri focused on a single thought: Lysa would be able to help. She had to get back to Lysa. Stacia was depending on her.

Still, it was taking all her willpower not to dissolve into sobs.

As she pulled Stacia down the hallway back toward the mess hall, a burst of static came in her headpiece, making her twitch and turn, her wrist light scanning wildly all around her.

"Chavri, Chavri please, please answer."

Lysa was sobbing. Chavri couldn't blame her.

"Lysa, I'm here. I have Stacia. She's not conscious, but I have her. I have her. We're both here." Chavri caught her breath, the warning signal in her suit beeping and telling her to slow her breathing down, that she was using up too much air.

"Chavri, gods, Chavri, I thought you were gone."

"I'm here, I'm here." She kept focused on her breathing until the warning sounds stopped, her air consumption normalized.

"Stacia, is she...?" She could hear Lysa control her own breathing through the headpiece.

"I don't know, Lysa. She's not moving. She's not awake. I don't know what's wrong with her."

Chavri felt her anxiety rising again.

"Bring her here. Just focus on that. Just bring her here. We'll figure it out."

Since that was exactly what Chavri was hoping for, she nodded in response.

"I'm on my way."

"Ten seconds," Lysa said. Chavri closed her eyes, and squeezed her hands into fists in an effort to keep from screaming or crying. She didn't want the silence again. Not again.

"You can do this, Chavri." Lysa's voice was steady. "For Stacia."

"For Stacia."

And then, silence. Chavri forced her hands to relax and resumed her journey.

It took longer to get two floating bodies, only one of which was conscious, back through the mess hall and to the airlock. Chavri tried really hard to ignore certain things about Stacia during the journey, like the fact that she didn't seem to be breathing, and that her body seemed stiff and inflexible. Frozen, like the others. Chavri spent all her energy on keeping them both moving, telling herself over and over again that it was going to be alright, that Stacia was going to be fine, that Lysa would have the answers. Finally, she got into the airlock and waited for the air to depressurize.

She checked Stacia's suit. Everything seemed to be operating, and as far as she could see, there was nothing wrong with it. But as Chavri shone her light through the glass of Stacia's helmet, really looking at her face for the first time since finding her body, Chavri could see that something was coating her skin, the same orangish something she had seen on the other bodies in engineering.

It's going to be all right, she told herself. It's going to be all right.

Because if it wasn't—if the worst had happened and Stacia was actually dead—Chavri wasn't sure how she would ever function again.

Chapter 10

Lysa ran an instrument over Stacia's body, her face tightly controlled. She had to keep it together, for Chavri's sake.

"You said the others also were frozen like this?"

"All ten of them. All of them in engineering. And there were those vines."

"Did the vines have thorns?"

Chavri tried to remember. Now that she was thinking about it, she did see what looked like a fuzzy texture to the vine, something that could have been small sharp thorns.

"I never touched the vines," she said. "Not with my hands. I used my wrench to move them."

"Yeah, but could there have been thorns? Protrusions of any kind?"

"Yeah, I think so. Why?"

Lysa sighed, clipping the instrument in her hands back inside its holder on the wall.

"There is a very small puncture to her suit, down by her right hip. She probably bumped into something, something so small and sharp it got through the material of her suit. It got inside."

"I don't understand," Chavri said, shaking her head.

"The orangish stuff. I think it came from the vines," Lysa said.

"We need to take her helmet off, get the suit off, and get the stuff off her. If we do that, we can save her." Chavri started to pull at Stacia's helmet, her hands clumsy. Lysa grabbed her and pulled her back.

"No, you don't understand. It's inside her suit. If we take her suit off, it can get in here."

"What, what can get in here?"

"The fungus."

"Fungus?"

Chavri shook her head. Panic was rising in her again, panic that she had managed to mostly keep at bay while she was focused on getting Stacia back to *Aurora Three*, while she was waiting for the airlock to pressurize, while she was telling Lysa everything she saw now that they were back in open communications range. All she had wanted was to get Stacia back to Lysa, so that Lysa could tell her that Stacia would wake up and she would be fine.

But Stacia wasn't fine. She wasn't fine, and Chavri was going to lose her, and this was all her fault.

"She went there because of me," Chavri said, choking on a sob. "Because of the metal. For me. Please, please. She has to wake up. What can we do? What do we do? How do we make her better?" The alarm sounds in her suit were going off again, her breathing erratic.

Lysa put her hands on either side of Chavri's helmet and held it steady, pulling Chavri close enough that Chavri's view was only of Lysa's face.

"She's alive. I don't know how. I don't know what's happening to her. But there are life signs. Subtle. But steady. She's alive. I need you to hear that. She's alive."

Chavri stared into Lysa's green eyes, Lysa's gaze an anchor in the storm of emotions she was experiencing.

Stacia was alive. It was enough for Chavri to use to steady her breathing, to focus her thoughts.

"You said fungus," she said at last, her mind catching up with the conversation.

"That's what the readings say," Lysa said, letting Chavri go while keeping a wary eye on her. "And there is something else— all the oxygen in her suit is gone."

"Wait, then how?"

"How is she still alive? I don't know. But the fungus isn't just on her. It's in her—in her lungs, like she breathed it in. I've been looking at the scans you sent back from the *Aurora One*. You said there was air there, right?"

"It pressurized the airlock."

"Yeah, but that is pumped in from an internal system. That comes from tanks. The rest of the place, everywhere else you traveled? I don't think there was any oxygen in that air."

"Why?"

"I think the fungus feeds on it. And then puts out nitrogen."

"Nitrogen?" Chavri shook her head, trying to make sense of what Lysa was saying. She looked back at Stacia, her hand reaching out to touch the closest part of her. It was then that she noticed a small patch of what looked like orange powder on Stacia's hip.

"Lysa?"

She pointed. Lysa whipped out her scanner and waved it over the area, and as they both watched, the patch of something vaguely orangish grew. And kept growing.

"Chavri, move back!" Lysa stepped back herself, still scanning, still trying to figure out what was happening.

The orange powder had mass now, thickening into structures that looked very like the vines that Chavri had found on the *Aurora One*.

"We have to get that off her!" She tried to go to Stacia, but Lysa held her back.

"It's coming from her!" she said, dragging Chavri back with her. "We have to get out of here, get to the bridge, seal this part off."

Chavri hesitated, but as the vines kept growing, she saw that they were forming pustules that where exploding an orange substance into the air.

"Spores," Lysa said from behind her.

Chavri couldn't believe how fast the spores were spreading. The door to the airlock was now covered in vines, and the orange powder from the spores was coating everything. Several places where they landed they seemed to sprout more vines that clung to the electrical panels. Chavri turned toward Lysa then, finally ready to flee with her to the bridge.

Then she wrenched her hand out of Lysa's in shock and horror. Lysa was covered in the same orange powder—the spores she had tried to warn Chavri about. Her eyes were open, staring at Chavri, but they were coated too. And she wasn't moving. Not her hands, not her chest, not even her hair. She was frozen, just like the people on the *Aurora One*, just like Stacia.

Chavri looked down and saw the outside of her space suit coated in the same orange substance.

The alarm beeps of her suit alerted her to the fact that she was probably hyperventilating, and she closed her eyes and focused on slowing down her breath, creating a plan of action. She had an independent air source, she reminded herself. She would fly the *Aurora Three* out of the asteroid belt. She would call for help. She would go back to L'Mondeau. The doctors there would fix this. This was fixable. She could still fix everything.

Chavri opened her eyes. Everywhere she looked there were more vines. She pulled out her wrench and used it to push them away, turning around to make her way to the bridge, trying to find a path free enough of the vines. She shoved off from the nearest panel and floated forward, trying to outrun the vines.

Then she felt it. A snag, down by her left knee.

Zero gravity meant that any object in motion stayed in motion, and her momentum carried her forward so that the snag became a tear. She couldn't bend down to see it, but she felt it, felt the pressure in her suit change. All the alarm bells in the suit were blaring, and a voice said calmly, "Suit integrity has been compromised."

"No no no no no!" Chavri chanted to herself. She tried to break free of the vine that punctured her suit, yanking her leg away, but she could already no longer feel her left knee. She managed to pull back, but now she couldn't feel her left foot either, and her right hip was starting to go numb. She tilted her head forward as far as her helmet would allow, and could just barely see down her torso inside her suit. She watched as the orange spores traveled up her body, felt them move down her sleeves as she lost feeling in her arms and hands, and then felt the same cold numbing sensation hit her shoulders, and her neck.

"No!" she yelled. She took a last breath and tried to hold it in, tried not to breathe in the spores, but they were on her face, clouding her vision, filling her nose, and she couldn't hold her breath any longer, and let it out with a final scream.

Then the spores were inside her mouth, and down her throat.

Then she wasn't aware of feeling anything at all.

PART IV:

The Prince

Now, it so happened that a Prince arrived in these parts. He was the son of a king in a country close by. Young, handsome and melancholy, he sought in solitude everything he could not find in the company of other men: serenity, sincerity and purity. Wandering on his trusty steed he arrived, one day, at the dark forest. Being adventurous, he decided to explore it.

Classic Fairy Tales, The Sleeping Princess

Chapter 11

Riku Dvorak ducked behind the twisted trunk of a large tree, his plasma rifle up by his side, and tried to stay as still as possible. Times like these, he wished his bright red hair didn't stand out quite so much or that he wasn't so vain so that he could just shave it off. The patrol passing on the road below him was closer than he had thought they would be, and he felt the fear and paranoia of being taken by surprise, immediately followed by the anger and shame of not having anticipated their movements better. He looked back and the rest of his unit had also managed to find cover, apparently in time, since there was no unusual sound from the patrol below them that indicated his unit had been seen.

Thank the gods for small favors, he thought. *Now gods, stay with us.*

Riku lowered himself down as low as he could and carefully peeked around the edge of the tree. The patrol was a least the anticipated size, and the anticipated level of armed, although he couldn't help but sneer at the rifles the group held.

The Thirteenth were supposed to abhor all things technological and fought to bring the people of L'Mondeau back to a more basic, less environmentally impactful way of living. And yet this patrol group was armed with the latest design of plasma rifles, likely the same ones that had been stolen during the raid on the Durrantian transport three weeks back.

Riku had an inbred hatred of The Thirteenth, as one of their first terrorist acts took out a relative of his back in the realm of King Ardan on the naming day of the King's one and only heir.

Two decades later, they had claimed responsibility when Princess Chavri's spaceship never came back. After that, it seemed the The Thirteenth felt emboldened on a whole new level, and terrorist attacks against the Twelve Provinces became common.

Mehmtok stopped supporting Moarga soon after, as apparently they had hoped to marry the Moargan princess off to one of the Merchant Princes in their province in a move that would have expanded their territory into Moargan space. Without an alliance by marriage, they withdrew their support from the largest province of L'Mondeau. After all, there was no profit in defending Moarga, so they invested instead in a wall along the edge of the Harbin Mountain range, focusing on keeping The Thirteenth out through border security. That left Moarga, on the other side of the mountain range, to become the favorite target of the The Thirteenth. Generations later, the stronghold of The Thirteenth had expanded well into Moargan territory, and what had started as a series of skirmishes had become all-out war.

Riku had seen the vids of the death of his great great Aunt Eva when he came of age, and the image of her flesh melting as she did her best to block a noxious gas from escaping the enemy's bio weapon still haunted his nightmares.

Riku waited until most of the patrol had passed, putting his unit behind him, and then tapped his coms device twice to signal everyone to move in. They all went as quietly as they could, staying under cover until they got to the very edge of the road. Once in position, Riku tapped in another command, waited for a count of ten, and then stood up and fired his plasma rifle at the target he had picked out on his way down toward the patrol. The

Thirteenth soldier fell instantly, along with a half a dozen more before the rest of the unit even got a chance to turn around with their guns up. Their commander was shouting at them to take cover, but Riku and his unit advanced forward, still enjoying the cover of the forest and higher ground, and managed to take out another swatch of the patrol before they got organized enough to return fire with any efficiency.

Riku turned and ran through the woods toward the front of the patrol group, keeping an equal eye on the enemy commander and the path ahead of him, stalking his target much as he imagined a predator would. The commander was ensconced behind a wall of his soldiers, the coward, and Riku felt confident that if he fell, the rest of the group would surrender. Finally spotting an opening, Riku jumped down a small ridge, landing with his rifle at his shoulder, and fired a steady stream of plasma fire directly at the center. Two soldiers fell trying to protect the commander before Riku's plasma fire hit him square in the face, and he went down with half his flesh burned off. Riku's unit was emerging from the woods on both sides of the road the patrol unit had been travelling, and the remaining Thirteenth soldiers threw themselves flat on the dirt, hands behind their heads, unprompted. Those were the smart ones. The ones that tried to keep their guns or fire back fell dead.

"Status!" Riku said into his communicator. Daniel, who was covering things behind them, was the first to respond:

"All clear."

"Clear up here," Emily said. Intel had been right then that this patrol was out on their own. Riku's group was gathering up all the weapons of The Thirteenth soldiers on the ground, dead or alive. Once they were clear, Riku pointed his gun at what looked to be the highest ranked Thirteenth solider still alive.

"Up," he said. The soldier complied, keeping her hands behind her head and getting up slowly from her knees. "By order of Queen Laney of Moarga, you are under arrest for acts of terrorism. You will be assigned counsel, and given housing and food while you await travel. If you have any loved ones, they will be notified of your status. Do you have any questions?"

She blinked as though she hadn't fully understood what he said.

"You're arresting us?"

"You're criminals." He kept his rifle steady and watched her closely. She looked down at the bodies strewn over the road, and the few others that were still alive, and then back at Riku.

"You ambushed us."

"You're on Moargan land. We defended it, and now we're arresting you."

She stared at him for a long moment.

"You won't just kill us?" she asked.

Riku sighed. That's the thing about terrorists, he thought. *They always think your side is as bad as theirs.*

"We don't kill prisoners. And the moment you put down your gun, that's what you became. We didn't start this," he said, using his gun to point out the bodies littered around them. "But we do intend to finish it. Now, officially, do you surrender?"

The woman looked uncomfortable, obviously still not convinced, but she nodded anyway.

"Yes, on behalf of the remaining Thirteenth here, I officially surrender."

"Good," Riku said. Everything had gone about as well as it could have. Except for the part where a bunch of people were dead, even if they were the enemy.

Chapter 12

Prince Ardan ran his hand over his bare head, a habit he picked up somewhere between receding hairline and might-as-well-just shave-it-all-off. He was now fully smooth, and not particularly unhappy about it—one less thing to worry about. He was wiry, seeming to get thinner and harder as he aged in direct contrast to many of the other men his generation, who had a tendency to get soft and round. He walked with a slight limp, the stabilizers in his mechanical leg having gone out of alignment, and supported himself with the help of a cane. While he had inherited the famous Aisling blue eyes from his mother's side, he'd also inherited her tendency to burn, his light brown skin taking on a sepia tone due to too much time in the sun, and deep lines forming around his eyes. He worried about the lines and all other indicators that he was getting older, not because he feared aging, but because he feared what Riku might think.

"How'd he look?" he asked Eural as they walked toward Riku's chambers.

"Tired," she said.

Eural Mellon was a lively woman with blonde-hair-turning-white and almost as many years in the field as Ardan had. She'd been in his unit in his war days, as he called them, and had specifically requested to be transferred back to the capital after her mother fell ill. He'd granted that request, not knowing that a year later he'd be back in the capital himself, burying his last siblings two months after Eural buried her mother. He was glad to have her in his entourage. She understood life as a soldier, and had enough knowledge of court to help him with politics. Plus, she had been Riku's commanding officer at one point, and both liked him and liked taking him down a notch, as needed.

"He's likely bruised all to shit," Ardan complained to her as they walked.

"Sounds right," she said. "Still pretty, though. I checked for you."

"That's not the point."

Of all the things he thought his life might hold falling in love with his personal guard wasn't one of them. Being the last surviving heir of the Aisling royal line also wasn't one of them, but there wasn't much he could do about that either.

A hallway length later, Ardan sighed deeply and tried again. "I miss him when he's gone."

"As you should. And still he will go. You know that, same as I do. He's too young to put up his rifle, not while The Thirteenth continues to attack the way they do."

The Thirteenth had been trying to wipe out the Aisling family since the days of King Ardan, who he was named for. But generations of warfare had left only two Aislings left in the world—him and his aging-but-spry mother, Queen Laney. He'd had two older brothers and a younger sister. In the last twenty years, he had lost them all, along with his father, and part of his leg. That made him the official heir, and brought him out of the field and into court, a transition he was none-too-pleased about.

"If only we'd had Mehmtok on our side. Or even Durrant. They've all abandoned us."

"They're all scared, and dealing with their own attacks."

"Selfish, all of them. Moarga always went to their aid. We still do."

"Yes," Eural agreed. "We have that Moargan honor. And where has it gotten us?"

Ardan whirled around to face her.

"That was borderline blasphemous," he said, leaning heavy on his cane.

"The truth often is," she replied, her gaze steady. He harrumphed at her with an exaggerated sound. She indulged his grumpy old man routine more than most, and he always enjoyed their exchanges.

"You're very like my mother," he said.

"Whoa now, that's just going too far. I thought you liked me?"

Ardan laughed, turning back around and resuming their course. His mother, Queen Laney, was well past the age of retirement, but had no notion of slowing down. She was a hard-edged woman with a sharp mind and sharper wit, and Ardan admired her deeply. But she was not an easy person, even if she was an excellent ruler.

"I can pick someone else," he said to Eural. "Give him the rest he is long due."

"He'd never forgive you," Eural said. "And he'd rather be with you, then resting."

Ardan nodded, and knocked on Riku's door.

"Enter," he heard him call, and went inside while Eural stayed outside, taking guard.

Riku made a feeble attempt to stand and bow, which Ardan

waved off, and then sat back on his bed again. His curly red hair was a matted mess on his head, and his nose and cheeks were red, a sunburn making his freckles pop out. He had visible bruises on his bare arms, and Ardan could only guess at what the rest of him looked like.

"You were out a long time," Ardan said.

"It wasn't a good trip," Riku said. "We lost five, killed over three dozen, and captured around twenty. Too many dead." He rubbed his face with his hand, disturbing a raw scab just under his hairline in the process. "Shit," he said.

Ardan limped over to him and grabbed his chin in a firm grasp, tilting his head up to look at the cut. "Stay still," he ordered, then took a scanning instrument from the pouch on his belt and waved it over Riku's face. "It's not deep, just bloody."

He pulled another instrument from his belt, and bracing his legs so that he could lean his cane against the bed, took Riku's face in one hand and pointed the tool at the cut on his forehead with the other.

"There, all better," Ardan said. He bent down and kissed Riku's lips in a short but sensual kiss before settling down next to him. Riku leaned into Ardan's side and Ardan put his arm around Riku's shoulder.

"We don't have long," Ardan said quietly. "I'm supposed to be debriefing you on our next mission."

"Our?" Riku asked.

"There was a discovery, an object, in space."

"Metal source?"

"In a manner of speaking. It seems to be a space ship."

Riku sat up straight and turned to Ardan.

"The Aurora," he said.

"One of them. Maybe. The Queen wants to send a team to investigate. You and Eural are the only ones who completed your space simulation trainings."

"You're going," Riku said accusingly.

"We don't have any spaceships," Ardan replied. Riku sighed.

"Mehmtok."

"And Declan. Which means I have to go. Besides, if I'm there, I can officially claim whatever it is in the name of Moarga."

"If it's a ship, it's already Moarga's," Riku said.

"You really think Declan wouldn't try to claim it anyway?"

"What does he get out of this deal?"

"Not marriage, if that's what you're worried about," Ardan said, running his hand lightly up and down Riku's back. "Not that people are comfortable yet with same-sex royal marriages any-way—they get weird about the lineage, as if royals of old weren't more likely than not born from secret surrogates. Although, really I don't know why they don't think we'd be just like everyone else. But no, it turns out that Declan has his own reasons for going into space—he'd already been planning a trip. This way part of the cost gets covered by us. And if there is a discovery, he wants the glory of helping find it."

Riku leaned against Ardan.

"Sounds typical," he said. He turned his head and nuzzled into Ardan's shoulder.

"We don't have to leave now, do we?"

"Tonight," Ardan said. "Declan is apparently in a hurry to go.

The Queen is too." Riku's entire body sighed. "You don't have to go," Ardan said. "You just got back, and you could use the rest."

"If you're going, I'm going," Riku said. "Especially if Declan is involved."

Ardan chuckled, pleased that Riku could still feel a little jealousy, even if it was completely irrational.

"We have a little time though," Ardan said.

"Good," Riku said. He shifted into a more comfortable spot, leaning heavily on Ardan. "It was a hard trip," he said quietly.

Ardan kissed the top of Riku's head, and ran his hand through Riku's hair, gently untangling it.

"I know, my love. And I'm sorry."

Chapter 18

Dr. Nahaila Haider was staring up at a projection of the Kuntak Asteroid Belt when Riku and Ardan found her. She was dictating a string of numbers and positions into a pad. After a moment, Riku recognized them as the paths of various asteroids in the belt, along with something else that seemed to be snuggled up against one of the largest shapes.

"Is that the object?" he asked. Dr. Haider glanced his way but didn't stop her recitation. If she noticed the royal prince next to Riku, she gave no indication. Riku exchanged a look of amusement with Ardan.

Dr. Haider was of an age to the prince, with streaks of grey in her long brown hair. She wore a *dupatta* lightly around her shoulders, and a *shalwar kameez* below that—essentially a long tunic over baggy trousers that were tapered at the ankle. Dress like this had become popular during Queen Sulina's time. Dr. Haider looked like she could have been related to Queen Sulina and Riku wondered if that was in fact the case. Sulina was from Durrant, a second sister, and had originally been promised to a merchant prince of Mehmtok. Then she met King Ardan. Her family came around to the idea, though some reports suggested they didn't really have a choice. Queen Sulina was said to be strong willed and opinionated. It was known that she served as an equal ruling partner to King Ardan, never content to sit back and play a passive role of consort. It was said their daughter had many of her mother's traits, and that it was a great loss to Moarga that she never ascended to the throne.

Riku often wondered how history may have changed if Princess Chavri had become queen. The Thirteenth seemed determined to ensure that never happened, and eventually succeeded. Riku couldn't help feeling it was a great loss to the province.

Dr. Haider finally completed her recitation, ordering the computer to compile the results, and turned to face her guests.

"Yes," she said. "That is an object. I would need more information before I was able to tell you if it was 'the' object. Which object were you referring to?"

Ardan made a slight bow of apology.

"Forgive us, Doctor. We have just come from the Queen and were anxious to begin the task she set for us. We were told that a metal object had been found in the Kuntak, and that you would be able to provide us with more information about it. We were also told you would be accompanying us to inspect the object."

Dr. Haider, for her part, seemed to finally catch on to who exactly was addressing her, and hastily executed a clumsy curtsy.

"Prince Ardan," she said. "I didn't…"

"I was not announced," he replied, waiving off her demonstration of reverence. "And I am too much soldier to care much for ceremony. You will call me Ardan, Doctor. These are my attendants, who will be accompanying us on this task: Riku Dvorak and Eural Mellon. Now, what do you know about this object?"

Dr. Haider paused for a moment, glancing at Riku and Eural as though to try to get more information about how to proceed. Both just smiled at her pleasantly, but that seemed to reassure her. She stopped curtseying and went back to her computer projection.

"Well, I do not think it is a natural phenomenon. So that leaves three possibilities," she said, zooming the projection onto the vague shape huddled by the asteroid. "There are two ships from L'Mondeau who have ventured out to the Kuntak, and both went missing after they did: *Aurora One*, from King Liam's reign, and *Aurora Three* from King Ardan's. The third possibility is that this is a ship, or probe, or other type of space vehicle from one of the other colonies."

Ardan stepped forward with keen interest, and Riku exchanged a surprised look with Eural.

"It that actually a possibility?" Ardan asked.

"I suppose it could also be some sort of vehicle or probe from an alien species, or something one of the other provinces put up there in secret, but in terms of probability, I believe this is either *Aurora One*, *Aurora Three*, or from another colony, as they at least might have reason to seek out L'Mondeau."

Riku understood more clearly why the Queen would send her son and only heir on a mission like this. The stakes suddenly seemed higher.

"What I do know is that this particular asteroid, number Q5432, as discovered and categorized by Dr. Rago, is a C-type and has a large enough mass to create a gravity well powerful enough to keep this object next to it," Dr. Haider continued. "That's the good news."

"What's the bad news?" Eural asked, getting directly to the point.

"Communication," the doctor replied. "Something about

that asteroid in particular seems to interfere with scans. We were lucky to get the information we did. But I am also certain that our communication will be compromised once we're up there. I am not certain how much so."

"We can deal with that issue when we get to it," Ardan said. "How soon could you be ready to head to Mehmtok?"

"In the hour, if need be."

"Not as soon as that. We'll head out tonight." The pass to Mehmtok was always dangerous, but cover of dark helped them more than The Thirteenth. Riku wished they had the capacity to build safe flying machines, like they had back on Earth, but with limited metal on the planet, and most of it too soft to offer any real protection, they were stuck using land vehicles, which used a combo of stone and force fields to keep their occupants safe. They sacrificed speed for protection, but Riku thought it was the better trade off.

"We'll meet after dinner," Ardan said.

"I'll continue to look for a solution to our communication problem until then," Dr. Haider said.

She turned back to her pads and was already deep in thought. Riku suppressed a laugh at Ardan's look of mild annoyance. He talked big about not caring for the reverence afforded to him by his title, but Dr. Haider's obvious obliviousness was definitely getting to him. Ardan seemed lost for a second, and then turned and headed out of the lab. Riku grinned at Eural, who was equally amused, before taking his place in front of Ardan, moving quickly to get ahead of the prince, while Eural took her spot behind them.

"She's certainly an odd one," Ardan said once in the hallway.

"I like her," Eural said.

"You would," Ardan replied. Riku didn't even bother to hide his laughter at his beloved and was rewarded by a very un-princely snort.

"I get no respect," Ardan complained. As the trio passed two guards stationed outside a hallway leading to the main part of the capital building, both guards saluted. Prince Ardan gave them each a nod of recognition, but they held their salutes until he passed.

Eural waited until the guards were out of hearing range before commenting:

"Nope, no respect at all."

Chapter 14

Dr. Haider clutched her satchel close in to her body, whether to protect it or get protection from it, Riku couldn't tell. They were five hours into a seven hour journey to Mehmtok through the Harbin Mountains, and while they were making good time, the journey was anything but smooth. The Mehmtokians had created a series of tunnels through the range with powered roads in many sections that helped vehicles go faster than on their own. Without that technology, the journey would take substantially longer. Even with them, the journey was rough, with the vehicles rocking back and forth like ships at sea.

Riku was just glad that the The Thirteenth hadn't blocked one of the tunnels or ripped up the transit panels, as they had in the past. It probably meant they were using them, which was its own worry, but at least there was a chance that the Moargans could make it to Mehmtok without incident.

"I have never come this way," Dr. Haider said. "Is it always like this?"

"Not at all," Eural said from her spot next to Riku. "Usually it's much worse."

Dr. Haider's eyes grew big and she clutched her satchel closer.

"This is the worst of it," Riku assured her. She nodded back, and put one hand up to the roof of the vehicle to help steady herself.

Ardan was in the seat in front of Eural, an additional force field separating him from the others in the vehicle. Three of Riku's best soldiers accompanied them: Mack, driving the vehicle; Daniel, covering Mack in the front compartment; and Emily, sitting in the turret at the top of the vehicle, sweeping the vehicle's gun all around in a regular scan of the surrounding territory. He'd asked for volunteers. He wasn't surprised when his entire unit raised their hands. He picked these three because they were the most senior and had the most experience.

"Update?" he said into his communicator.

"Still clear," Emily said.

"Clear up here," Daniel added.

Riku nodded. He trusted them to notify him as soon as they saw anything, but regular check ins also made sure that they hadn't been hit by sniper rifle. He'd once been in a vehicle with a turret gunner who'd been dead for about six hours before anyone had found out. Ardan, his unit leader in the time back when he wasn't the official heir, instituted a regular fifteen minute check in policy after that.

Riku could tell that Ardan was frustrated to be behind the force field, but that was also a policy he had put in place in an effort to protect his siblings and other high ranking officials. The inner force field had saved the life of at least half a dozen folks. Unfortunately, it wasn't enough to save Ardan's little sister on her journey to meet the merchant prince she was supposed to marry. The entire caravan had been attacked, and only six Moargans survived. Riku and four others had managed to get Ardan out—but the prince lost his leg from the knee down. He'd also lost his brother and sister, and became the last remaining Aisling heir.

Riku hoped he'd taken enough precautions.

"Mr. Dvorak, I wonder if you have any answer to the rumors that suggest that Mehmtok, or at least some of its merchant houses, may be backing The Thirteenth? Or that there may in fact be spies in Moarga, helping the movement."

Riku thought for a long moment, weighing out what to say to Dr. Haider.

"Or both," he said at last. Dr. Haider nodded, her look grave.

"That would explain a lot," she said. "We shouldn't be losing this war."

"We're not," Eural said sharply.

"We're not winning," Dr. Haider said gently. "I have lost family to The Thirteenth. And I started off my career working on counters to the biological weapons they use. We have been fighting them for generations, and every year they seem to get still more recruits, more people who believe firmly that the only way to save L'Mondeau and human kind is to wipe out any and all technology."

"And yet they use technology to do it." Eural looked like she wanted to spit. If they had been outside and in different company, Riku knew she would have—he'd seen her do it enough times.

"They are on what they feel is a holy mission. As such, they will use whatever they can to do what they believe is necessary. They are not hypocrites so much as fanatics. This is an ideological war. And the fact that The Thirteenth continue to exist, continue to grow in numbers year after year proves that on that front, we are losing. I wish it were not so. Truly."

She pulled a pendant out from under her tunic, and held it with her eyes closed for a moment, as though saying a short prayer. Riku caught Eural's eye to make sure she saw it. Eural had—she wore something very similar. Memorial pendants had become depressingly common over the past centuries.

"My son," Dr. Haider said at last, tucking her pendant back inside her tunic.

"He was killed by The Thirteenth," Eural said, nodding.

"He became The Thirteenth," Dr. Haider said, meeting Eural's gaze, not in challenge, but as though she was seeking some understanding. "I don't know if he is alive or not. But he is lost, just the same. Many have been—and we owe it to them to try to understand not just the how, but the why."

"Do you know why your son joined The Thirteenth?" Eural asked.

"He was a Naturalist, who struggled greatly with the idea of humans moving to new worlds, evolving and adapting to them, spreading humanity without any checks on their growth. And even with the most progressive environmental protection policies of all of L'Mondeau, he still felt that Moarga failed to push the other provinces hard enough to do the same. He felt that Moarga was responsible for the poverty of Mehmtok because they saw it and did not invade that province in an effort to stop it. Those who see the problem are responsible for solving it. I taught him that. I did not think that lesson would take him where it did."

Dr. Haider was quiet for a moment.

"As a scientist, I am sympathetic to the environmental cause of The Thirteenth. But I also see how they use that as an excuse to wage a war not against progress, but against diversity of thought. They claim they are trying to save the planet, but they also push for a dictatorship, for harsh punishment of any deviation from their ideals. I don't know how they became so radicalized. But I know that their message of false heroism seduced my son, gave him purpose and meaning and answered his doubts in a way I never could. Righteous belief is a heady narcotic, and those high on their own skewed morality are blind to their hypocrisy. My son could not see reason. And I could not see a way to get him back."

Riku's head immediately filled with questions, but one look at Ardan made him swallow them all. Eural for her part reached out a hand to Dr. Haider, who took it. The two women seemed to reach some sort of understanding then.

Riku looked at Ardan again, and he nodded lightly. He knew. Of course he would know. Ardan never worked with anyone he didn't thoroughly research. And if Ardan still trusted Dr. Haider, so would Riku.

But he was haunted by the idea that someone as reasonable as Dr. Haider could raise a son that could be lost to a terrorist organization. He felt a new hopelessness that The Thirteenth could ever be truly defeated.

Chapter 15

The group got into Mehmtok without incident, much to Riku's relief, and was greeted by their host, Declan Gould. The merchant prince was adorned in fine silks and jewels in the custom of the Mehmtokians to demonstrate their wealth through decoration, but also had a fighter's build and wary black eyes. Half-a-head shorter than Riku, he was denser and more muscled, easily out-weighing him. His personal guard and ship's pilot, Geoff, was even more impressive, and looked like he spent his off-time throwing boulders around. All the Mehmtokians dressed in sleeveless tunics with decorated arm cuffs indicating their house, and medallions indicating their rank within that house. Anyone looking at Declan would know his was the highest rank of the wealthiest house, just based on his jewelry alone.

The Mehmtokian scientist, Dr. Shawn Bernard, seemed cut from the same cloth as Geoff, broad and tall, younger than expected, and reserved in his speech and movement. He was from the southern region of Mehmtok, and wore his hair trimmed close to his scalp, the black curls left natural, as was popular there. His adornment was modest, and consisted of the customary Mehmtokian arm cuff and a single chain. He supervised the loading of equipment with a quiet authority that impressed Riku. He wasn't a warm man, but he was efficient, and that was a welcome contrast to Declan.

"Are you ready for the single greatest flight of your life?" Declan asked, gesturing to his ship. The Mehmtokian ship, the *Pres-*

tige, was in surprisingly good repair for something as old as it was. It was large, and built with an eye to design as well as function, the forward heat shield curved and the rest of the ship extending out from it like an upside down vase, narrower in the middle and bulbous at the end.

Riku looked over at Ardan, who nodded in return. Riku led the Moargans to the airlock at the rear of the ship, waiting for Declan and his group to enter first.

The airlock opened up to a small hallway lined with strapped down equipment, including space suits to accommodate ten crew members. To the left was engineering, an efficiently designed space that housed the fuel and air the crew would need. Across the way was another door, and Dr. Bernard went through it without a word. Riku didn't get a chance to question this as Declan lead the group forward toward the crew quarters. While the rest of the space was plain and functional, every part after was as gaudy as Declan himself. The crew cabins, such as they were, held large mattresses and were designed for more than sleeping. Riku had heard that guests on the *Prestige* had dalliances in space, but it seemed like a bad idea to him. Moving around in near zero gravity posed a lot of challenges—he couldn't imagine doing it while trying to interact intimately with another body.

The center most section looked more like a lounge than something that would go into space. Riku marveled at seeing richly woven throw cushions on a space ship, and seats whose restraints were decorated with beads. This space was populated by windows—as many as the designers could be persuaded to include, Declan said—all to suit a recreational trip to the stars.

Riku wondered idly how the pillows fared in zero gravity until a gentle tug on one of them revealed that it was attached to the seat below it by a thick thread wound about a button on the underside.

"They can be rearranged quite easily," Declan assured him with a look that made Riku's skin try to crawl away from the merchant prince. It was full of lust and longing, and seemed to be Declan's default expression.

"And the bridge?" Ardan asked. Declan waved dismissively toward the bow of the ship, the part protected by the heat shield outside.

Ardan nodded to Riku, who opened the door on that end and looked inside. It was a small, cramped space designed for two people to sit in. Riku explored the controls and various components and was satisfied that everything seemed to be in working order. He'd never actually been in a space ship before, but had spent enough time in the simulators to get an idea of how things should look. The Moargans firmly believed space flight would be part of their future again, with scientists exploring various other ways to build ships capable of breaking through the atmosphere and withstanding the radiation in space. The biggest issue had been weight—nothing they had been able to come up with was both as light and as strong as the metal the colonists came to L'Mondeau in. Riku took a moment to run his hand over the doorway back to the main part of the ship, marveling at the smooth durability of the metal.

They'd done well on a planet that seemed to lack this most basic Earth material. But they had spent their centuries on L'Mondeau trying to replicate the functionality and protection of technology they no longer had the means to recreate. They had to discover all new ways to conduct electricity and heat, to blend ceramic compounds that had a chance of being as strong and light as metal, to create manufacturing industries without steel or iron or aluminum. It had been a constant test of ingenuity.

There were those who had hoped to find significant enough sources of metal in the other astral bodies around L'Mondeau, people like the Princess Chavri, but after her ship was lost and the war with The Thirteenth truly began, people more or less gave up on the idea. Space flight had become all but extinct, and any dream of finding the other Earth colonies had died with it.

And yet Riku was standing in an actual space ship, on a mission to actual space.

"One of the last of her kind," Declan said, catching Riku's eye. "It's a shame, too. Once we get up there, you'll see. There is nothing quite like being among the stars. I feel privileged to have such a unique experience."

Riku studied Declan's face and saw that the man was genuine, at least in this.

"I am very much looking forward to the view," Riku offered. Declan smiled, a real smile, and Riku almost started to like him.

"There is more than the view to enjoy in space," Declan said. "Many new experiences can be had." He was back to his salacious grin, and Riku's view of him soured again.

"Riku," Ardan called, saving Riku from coming up with a response. He gave Declan a thin-lipped smile and carefully moved past him back to the main cabin.

Ardan raised an eyebrow at Riku's expression and Riku flicked his eyes back at Declan. Riku wasn't sure what Ardan saw over his shoulder, but it was enough to make Ardan grimace.

"Are you all right?" Ardan asked. Riku nodded. Ardan brushed Riku's sleeve so lightly that no one else could possibly have noticed, but it was enough for Riku to feel comforted.

Chapter 16

Liftoff on the *Prestige* was a noisy, rocky experience, and Riku clung to his restraints well after they broke the atmosphere, until he felt his body getting lighter, his arms and legs floating easily up. He'd done weightless training as well, but there was something different about the actual experience, perhaps knowing that there was no way to get back to gravity without flying home that made it both more entertaining and more off-putting.

Ardan pointed to the window behind Riku, and he undid his restraints so that he could turn to see out of it. For a second, he forgot to breathe—he was staring at L'Mondeau. Not an image of it, not a drawing of it, but the actual planet, big and beautiful and breathtaking. It was also moving away from them, or rather they were moving away from it, and Riku watched for a long moment as it appeared to grow smaller. He felt a sudden and deep feeling of homesickness he had not expected, and reached for Ardan's hand out of instinct. The prince held it, his palm calloused and warm. It was enough to make Riku feel anchored and less alone.

Over the next two days, Riku learned to like space flight less and less. While the view of stars outside the windows was at first thrilling, soon it just became another reminder how isolated and vulnerable the *Prestige* was. While the ship had seemed large enough when he first boarded it, soon Riku found the *Prestige* to be claustrophobically small. It didn't help that Declan was a constant presence, always trying to engage him in conversation filled with innuendo, giving him knowing looks whenever he got so much as an arm-length near Ardan.

Ardan, for his part, was the consummate politician, warding off any question too personal with practiced ease, and managing to be charming and engaging while doing so.

"You really should relax more," Declan said, and tossed a freed pillow toward Ardan. Weightlessness made it spin lazily in the space between them and gave Ardan ample time to easily dodge it.

"I appreciate the advice, but we're getting closer to the Kuntak," he said.

"We're off to see an object, not fight a war. This is a safe mission," Declan said. "You soldier types—so easily worked up."

"Indeed," Riku said. "I'm going to check with Dr. Haider on her progress."

Declan rolled his eyes and moved over to one of the couches, pulling himself into a set of restraints so that he could give the illusion of lounging. Riku was happy to leave him there as he pulled himself over to where Dr. Haider was and looked over her shoulder at the console she was working at.

"Any news?" he asked her.

"We're getting the same interference," she replied. "I no longer think it's coming from the asteroid though."

"Then where?"

"I think it's the object. It's putting something out, something that is messing with our technology. I can't pinpoint it."

"How badly? Can you work around it?"

"It's not interfering with anything, per se, except for communication. And yes, I can work around it, for the most part."

"Good. Have you seen Dr. Bernard?"

"He's in his lab," she said.

"The one we're not allowed in, and where he does things we're not allowed to know about, and which are the very reason why the Mehmtok wanted to go to space?"

"The Mehmtokians enjoy their secrets," she said. "We have kept a few of our own as well, over the years. Dr. Bernard seems a reasonably cautious man. I can think of any number of experiments I would like to conduct while in space, and I doubt whatever he is doing poses any actual harm to the rest of us."

"I wish I shared your confidence," Riku said. "How much longer until we get to the Kuntak?"

"Three hours," she said without looking up.

"Three hours," Riku echoed. "I'll be much happier when this is over with and we're on our way back home."

"I'm sure you will be," she said. "I'll be much happier once we can actually confirm what it is we have actually found." She sighed then and straightened up as though to stretch out some ache in her back. "I know that finding the *Aurora*, if that is what this is, won't actually change anything on L'Mondeau, but I can't help but feel that the right scientific discovery could unite the provinces, and in doing so, give us a better chance at ending the violence of The Thirteenth."

"I don't see how," Riku said, "though I know Ardan shares your view."

"Perspective," Dr. Haider said. "Right now we are an isolated planet fighting over limited resources. But the heart of our space program has always been about connecting to something beyond our planet, something bigger than any one province. It's about discovery, wonder, finding our place in the universe."

"The Thirteenth believe that we have overstepped our place, that we should return to simpler living."

"Yes, with simpler rules, and black and white questions with black and white answers. They want to eliminate all nuance from life and create rigid lines for people to follow. They talk about a return to an old way of life as though there was ever a stage in human existence where living was simple or easy. If they ever actually achieved their goals, they would see how humans have always been capable of misery, no matter what edict they follow. They fight progress because the fight gives them meaning. I don't even think they want what they say they want. They want the fight."

"And finding a lost space ship—either lost space ship—will make them not want that anymore?"

"I'm not interested in the ship itself," Dr. Haider said. "I'm interested in what it may have found before it got lost. Both *Aurora One* and *Aurora Three* were searching for something—metal, or a way to get beyond this solar system and connect with others. The Thirteenth have used these disappearances, and every failure of technology, as proof that exploration is both dangerous and pointless. They build a campaign on fear and hopelessness. Any proof of progress is a counter-message, a way to resist that fear. Whatever we find, it will inspire people, inspire their imaginations and sense of hope. And those will be people The Thirteenth can't convince, can't recruit, can't corrupt. Discovery is resistance."

"Beautifully said," Ardan said from behind them, and both Riku and Dr. Haider twisted to see him. "My mother would agree with you wholeheartedly, Dr. Haider."

"She has been an ardent supporter of my work," the doctor said, recovering her composure. "I have been very grateful."

"As we have for the work you do," Ardan said. He rested his hand on Riku's shoulder. "We're three hours out," he said. "I want to check in with Eural before we get to the Kuntak."

Riku nodded at him but waited a moment while Adan moved away.

"Dr. Haider, thank you," Riku said. "I have been struggling with seeing hope for an end to this pointless and enduring conflict. But I think I understand now what you're saying—soldiers won't win the war against The Thirteenth. But maybe scientists, artists, and humanitarians will."

"They are the only ones who can," Dr. Haider said.

Chapter 17

Ardan stared at a projection Dr. Haider set up for the group near her workstation with no small sense of wonder.

"So, just to be clear, it's not a ship," he said. "It's ships, plural."

"As far as I can tell," Dr. Haider said. "With the interference, it took being this close to even get this information. We'll be able to see them out the windows soon."

"*Aurora One* and *Aurora Three*. How is that even possible?"

"This asteroid is the largest mass out in this area of space. It drew at least one of the ships into its gravity well—both had centuries to get here."

"This feels like too much of a coincidence," Riku said.

"We know that the *Aurora Three* was investigating something in the Kuntak," Dr. Haider said. "I suspect that the *Aurora One* may have been the thing it came to investigate."

"And that whatever happened to the *Aurora One* may have happened to the *Aurora Three*," Dr. Bernard said.

"Or their crews," Riku said. He was getting a bad feeling.

"We should board them, investigate," Dr. Haider said.

"Something happened to two separate crews hundreds of years apart, and you think we should possibly set us up to share their fate?" Declan shook his head. "I won't risk my ship. I don't have to tell you that no one has the resources to build another."

"And yet we finally have the answer to two mysteries waiting for us to find," Ardan said. "How can we resist that?"

"They are Moargan mysteries," Declan said. "I feel fine resisting them."

"There are ways to preserve the safety of the *Prestige*," Dr. Bernard said. "And I have to admit that I too would like to explore these lost vessels. If nothing else than to recover the data from the *Aurora One*, which had the most advanced scanning equipment of any vessel that ever existed. If Moarga agreed to share any data recovered, I would suggest that it would be well worth the risk."

Declan glared at Dr. Bernard, who stared serenely back. The merchant prince was the first to look way. Ardan had half a mind to recruit Dr. Bernard to work for Moarga then and there.

"There is clear risk," Riku said. "But I can't imagine coming all this way and not returning with the tale of what happened to Princess Chavri all those years ago." Riku's great great grandfather had served as the princess's personal guard. He'd tried, unsuccessfully, to get a ship to try to find her when she never returned. But none of the other provinces, including Mehmtok, wanted to risk their ships after The Thirteenth took credit for the destruction of the last Moargan craft. Eventually the focus of the province switched to taking on The Thirteenth, and Riku's ancestor had to give up his investigation into Princess Chavri's disappearance. There would be something poetic about another Dvorak solving the mystery, once and for all.

"I want to go to the *Aurora Three*, and if possible, recover her body."

Ardan understood perfectly and shared Riku's desire.

"I may be able to recover data from the ship," Dr. Haider said.

"And I could go as the Mehmtok representative," Dr. Bernard said.

Declan considered the three people staring at him.

"I won't hesitate to leave you behind," he said.

"I doubt it will come to that," Ardan said, confident that he and Eural could take over the *Prestige* if they had to. As the others drifted off to take care of preparations, Ardan pulled Riku into a corner by the crew cabins.

"It's going to be all right," he told the prince.

"I'm pretty sure that's what I'm supposed to say. You're the one going off on the dangerous mission."

He pressed his palm to Riku's cheek.

"You'll make it back safe," he said. "That's an order."

Riku smiled and kissed the prince.

It was nowhere near as deep or long as he wanted, but then Ardan was getting used to that. Their relationship had been defined by stolen moments.

Chapter 18

Riku tried to remind himself that he could still breathe. The fact that his breath was the loudest sound he could hear didn't actually make him feel better. He fought the urge to rip his helmet off and focused on slowing down his heart rate—the suit made angry beeping noises anytime he took in air too quickly. He felt clumsy, his hands too thick and his peripheral compromised. He also had no weapons that would work both with the suit and with the reality of being in space. He settled for a small tool kit, including a wrench and a sharp pair of pliers, and hoped for the best.

Geoff had gotten the *Prestige* as close to the other two ships as possible, and positioned it so that they could get to and board each with relative ease. Riku and the doctors were getting ready to head to the *Aurora Three*.

So step one, solve the mystery of Princess Chavri. Step two, get *Aurora One* flying again. Step three, go home and continue the war against The Thirteenth.

None of these are good steps, Riku thought.

He waited while the others finished putting on their suits and tested their coms systems. Ardan insisted on being the primary on coms back on the *Prestige*, something Riku was grateful for. Eural would be staying with the prince. Geoff would stay on the bridge. Declan would be Declan. Riku was not excited to see what the merchant prince might get up to during the mission.

Finally, Dr. Haider, the last to get suited up, was done, and gave a thumbs up indicating that all systems checked out.

"Everyone on the same channel?" Ardan asked. A chorus of ayes greeted him. "Good. May the gods hold you," he said. "Depressurizing airlock."

It was a long wait while all the air got sucked out of the space they were in, and Riku tried not to think about how with every second he was becoming more and more reliant on his suit.

"Airlock depressurized," Ardan said. "You're clear to leave the *Prestige.*"

Dr. Bernard opened the outer door from a panel in the wall. Riku moved to the edge of the door and clipped the end of a rope to the top of the doorway. The *Prestige* was at a slight angle to the *Aurora Three* and he was going to have to aim carefully. Fortunately, the *Aurora Three* had a lot of exterior things to grab in case he overshot his mark. Riku steadied his breathing, and then pushed himself off the door as hard as he could. One part of his brain recognized that he was in open space, and was terrified and awed at the same time. But the rest of it was focused on his target, determined to survive the experience.

He was aimed too high, and twisted his body so that his hands could reach out and grab whatever he could. He felt his heart race and his suit start to beep at him about his air use, but he stayed focused on one thing only—grab something. Anything.

His body hit the side of the ship, and he splayed out, trying to hook whatever he could with any part of him. He knew, intellectually, that if all else failed he would be pulled back and could try again. But his instincts were screaming at him to grab something as though his life depended on it.

Finally, his right hand found a handle, grabbed it, and held on. His body pulled back the other way with enough force that he almost lost his grip, but he held on, finding another handle with his other hand. Finally, he was pressed against the hull of the *Aurora Three*, safe, and secure.

"Riku, you good?" Dr. Bernard asked

"I'm good," Riku said. "Just regrouping."

"Move down, toward your feet," Dr. Bernard said. "The hatch is that way."

"Roger," Riku said. He looked for handles and other things to grab, and slowly moved feet-first down the side of the ship. He had a moment of panic when his foot couldn't find anything before he realized he'd reached the hatch. He went hand over hand until the hatch was in front of him. He unclipped the rope attached to his suit and put it on a handle to the ship, connecting the *Aurora Three* to the *Prestige*. Then he clipped a second rope to the handle to ensure he wouldn't float away either.

At last, he hooked his feet under two handles that seemed built for the purpose, and turned the outer wheel of the airlock.

"Scans say it's pressurized," Ardan warned. "They weren't expecting outside visitors."

"Roger," Riku said, and braced himself before pulling the door open with a final tug. The air inside rushed out, knocking him back. His feet kept their hold, and while he flailed and felt stupid, he stayed safe. It was a quick moment, and then he was able to move into the airlock. The inner door was sealed, and the space between was dark. Riku shined his light all around, but could see nothing in the space that seemed amiss.

Riku turned himself and watched as Dr. Bernard latched a

ring onto the rope between the ships, and then guided himself over it, hand-over-hand. He made it easily and without incident, and then turned expectantly.

"Coming now," Dr. Haider said, and she clipped her own ring onto the rope and pulled herself along it. She misjudged the last leap, and Riku had to reach out to grab her hand to keep her from crashing into the side of the ship.

"Thanks," she said. "Let's keep going." She moved toward the door to the ship and took out a scanner, waving it all around.

"Anything?" Riku asked.

"Nothing more than we saw already. There is something odd about the atmosphere inside. There's air, but the oxygen levels… well, there doesn't seem to be any oxygen in the air. And there is something else, some mass, something that doesn't line up with what I know about ships."

"Do you think they took something on board?" Riku asked.

"Yes," Dr. Bernard said, making his own scans of the doorway. "But we won't know what until we get inside."

"Will the airlock pressurize?"

"Yes," Dr. Haider said. "There is a manual control. Here." She pointed to a lever at the side.

"Closing the outer door," Riku announced, moving as he spoke. It was easier to close than to open. Once the seal was good, he turned to face the others. "Door closed."

Dr. Haider pulled the lever, and immediately the area started to fill with air.

"I recommend we keep our suits on," she said. "For safety."

As much as Riku had wanted to take off his helmet before,

he had no such desire to do so now. Now that he was actually on *Aurora Three*, he appreciated just how much nicer the *Prestige* was. The *Aurora Three* was the analogue to the *Prestige*'s digital. Even though Riku knew it was smaller, he didn't expect it to feel so much smaller. The four of them fit easily in the airlock on the *Prestige*, while three bodies seemed to take up all the space on the *Aurora Three*.

As his sense of claustrophobia grew, Riku felt a new appreciation for Princess Chavri. She had gone to space on the *Aurora Three*, fifteen times according to the records. Fifteen times she had trusted this small and cramped ship to keep her safe. And fourteen times, it did.

The airlock pressurization completed.

"Let me," Riku said. The doctors made space for him, an awkward shuffle of bodies, and Riku found his way to the inner door. It was another wheel, and he braced himself, and turned. He felt the click that indicated he had completed all the rotations and then pulled the door open.

The door snagged. As soon as Riku felt resistance, he stopped pulling. But the door kept moving anyway, some force on the other side pushing it open.

"Get back!" he yelled. The doctors pushed themselves far back as they could, but there wasn't a lot of back to go. Riku watched in horror as a vine snaked itself around the door, continuing to grow and stretch toward him and the doctors. He pulled himself as flat against the side of the airlock as he could.

"What is it?" he asked.

"It's a fungus of some kind," Dr. Haider said. "It's reacting to something in the air. Oxygen, it's reacting to the oxygen. Just wait."

She had a scanner out and was reading the results.

"Oxygen levels are falling rapidly. It will run out soon."

The vine continued to stretch out until it touched the outer door, growing thicker instead of longer until it was as thick as Riku's arm and the same tapered shape. Finally, it was still.

"All the oxygen in the area is gone," Dr. Haider said. "Remarkable! And the nitrogen levels are up. This is fascinating indeed."

"Agreed," Dr. Bernard, said moving closer to get better scans of the vine. Riku shook his head. Only scientists could find a terrifying moment fascinating.

"It is definitely a fungus," Dr. Haider announced. "But not a species I have ever encountered before."

"What sort of fungus grows vines?" Riku asked.

"It's not a vine," Dr. Haider said. "It's a hypha. Think fingers. Fungus grow from the tips of their hyphae, generally toward something—food or a chance for reproduction. These grew tremendously fast."

"It's part of a larger organism," Dr. Bernard added in. "The mycelium seems to have wound itself throughout this section of the ship. Think 'root network' although that is not accurate." He scanned the length of it until he got to the door, and then pointed his scanner inside the ship. "And there is something else. Some other objects. Dr. Haider?"

"Bodies," Dr. Haider said, coming up behind him. "Human. Three of them. Only…this can't be right."

She moved closer to Dr. Bernard so that he could see the readout on her arm.

"Are you seeing this?"

"That's not possible," he said simply. They both took more scans, typed things into their pads, showed their pads to each other.

Riku waited as long as his patience, curiosity, and fear would allow.

"What is it?" he asked.

"Life signs," Dr. Bernard said, annoyed by the interruption.

"The organism?"

"Human life signs," Dr. Haider said. She looked up from her pad and stared through the door, shining her light as far as she could see. Mostly it shined on more of the same type of vine. "We need to get in there. We need to know, for sure."

"Past the space mushroom?" Riku asked.

"Fungus," Dr. Haider corrected. "There were over 5.1 million species of fungus categorized on Earth, and an additional 1.4 million unique species found on L'Mondeau. This organism is not like any of those, but has many of the same properties. And it's big—it has three distinct parts, including vine-like out-grow-ings, the hyphae, which is what this is." She gestured at the hypha between them.

"What do we do?" Riku asked.

"Go in," Dr. Bernard said, exasperated. "Scan the fungus. Get a sample. And apparently, find those bodies." Dr. Bernard moved toward the door, pulling himself through it.

Riku knew he should object—he was the guard, after all, and

he should go first. But he felt like he lost his need to command the moment fungus came into the picture. The doctor pulled a tool from a pocket, and extended it to its full length, using it to move other floating hyphae out of the way.

Riku followed closely and shone his light over what was revealed. The fungus, if that's really what it was, seemed concentrated on a single spot in the middle of the space, some sort of mass that he couldn't quite make out. The hyphae, which really did look like vines, seemed mostly wound around or resting on technology, particularly anything that might have given off heat. Everything else seemed to be coated with a fine dust of something that Riku couldn't quite make out and definitely didn't want to touch.

Dr. Bernard didn't seem to have that issue, and was gathering a sample of the dust into a container.

"Spores, I think," he said.

Dr. Haider was keeping a more respectful distance, letting her instrument scan things before getting near them.

"There, in the middle. One of the life signs." She pointed to where the vine things seemed to converge. Riku moved forward and tried to get a better angle with his light, and almost jumped back when he saw a booted foot.

"It's a person," he said. "Dead. They have to be."

"I'm telling you, I'm getting life signs. And those aren't the only ones."

Dr. Haider turned to the left, her scanner directing her light.

"There!" she said. A second body, a woman by the likes of it, had snagged on a vine back toward what looked like might have been the engineering section of the ship.

"And there," Dr. Haider said, shining her light in the opposite direction. It lit up a figure in a space suit, floating up near the doorway that would likely lead to the bridge. This one was not caught up in any vines.

"We can grab that one," Dr. Haider said. "Take it with us. Then figure out how to deal with the fungus, maybe free the others."

Riku moved toward the body. "What do I need to know about this fungus?"

"It has spikes," Dr. Haider said. "Avoid them and you should be fine."

Riku pressed a series of commands into his suit that caused additional lights in his helmet, boots, and belt to light up. He took out his wrench and then looked over at the long tool that Dr. Bernard was holding.

"Can I use that?" he asked. The doctor handed it over.

It was tricky moving through the room without snagging any vines. They had large thin spikes sticking out of them and Riku had to move extra slowly to avoid them. The doctors helped, and kept their own lights shining in the direction Riku was going in.

"To your right," Dr. Haider said, and Riku pushed a vine away.

"Watch your left knee," Dr. Bernard said.

Riku made it to the body. He turned it around, careful not to snag it or himself on any spikes. As the helmet came into view, Riku felt a mixture of apprehension and sadness. Then he saw the face. Chavri Aisling was unmistakable—her portrait hung in a prominent part of the palace, and every Moargan was familiar with it. Riku clipped a short rope to Chavri, and looped the other end of it around his hand.

The doctors continued their instructions, and it wasn't long before Riku was passing the body over to Dr. Bernard and pulling himself through the airlock.

"What now?" he asked. It was going to be impossible to close the door while the vine was in the entry way.

"We cut it," Dr. Bernard said, pulling yet another tool out of his satchel and unfolding it to reveal an impressively sharp blade.

"Will it react?" Riku asked.

"It's a fungus, not an animal," Dr. Haider said. Still, Riku tensed up as Dr. Bernard sliced into the vine. Nothing happened, except that after some effort, he cut through. Riku let out a breath, and as quickly as possible, shoved the door closed. The vine end floated in toward the back door, and Dr. Haider gently shoved it to one side. She was focused now on the body Riku had rescued, staring at the face.

"I don't understand," she said at last. "I swear I am detecting life signs, but certainly she looks dead."

"Has her suit been compromised?" Dr. Bernard asked. He and Dr. Haider did a through inspecting, finding a tear in the suit near the left knee. Dr. Bernard pulled out a patch kit, and sealed it.

"What's the point?" Riku asked.

"Contamination," Dr. Bernard said. "There are spores throughout her suit. We'd rather they didn't get out."

"The spores are the life signs, right?"

But the doctors didn't say anything.

Riku flipped the lever that would suck the air out of the airlock, and waited for it to be depressurized. In the cramped space, it was impossible to avoid Chavri's body and the free-floating vine section, and he opted to focus on avoiding that instead. As the air was sucked out of the room, the vine began to whither. Both doctors made scans of it, Dr. Bernard scraping a sample of it into a container.

"It appears to need atmosphere, like us," Dr. Haider said. Riku was silently relieved.

Finally, their scans confirmed that the airlock was depressurized. Riku opened the outer door and helped Dr. Bernard clip Chavri's body to the line connecting the two ships. He pushed the vine segment which now looked like a dried-out tree branch into open space and was not sorry to see it float away. Dr. Bernard went across the rope first, dragging Chavri's body behind him. Then Dr. Haider, and then Riku. He left the rope connected.

He had a feeling they might be coming back to the *Aurora Three.*

Chapter 19

It took some effort, and several hours, but the second airlock on the *Prestige* had been turned into a makeshift science lab. Riku took the body there from the outside of the ship, strapping it in and sealing the outer door. Dr. Bernard had allowed Dr. Haider into his lab in the back of the *Prestige*, which Riku discovered had its own double-door entrance and capability of being completely sealed off from the rest of the ship, with an independent air source. That made Riku feel better about whatever experiments they were conducting. Their goal was to figure what, if anything, might kill the fungus so that they could rescue the other bodies. Riku grew more and more restless while waiting for results from the experiments, watching the time pass by with an eye to their remaining air and energy reserves.

"We can't keep this up much longer," he said to Ardan in the privacy of the prince's cabin. "It's still a two-day journey back."

"I know," Ardan said. "But I'm not going back without the princess, and we can't take her back until we figure out how to control the fungus covering her body."

Ardan stroked Riku's arm absently, his mind elsewhere.

"What else?" Riku asked. "What else is bothering you?"

"Dr. Bernard. He seems to know a lot about poisons and such, don't you think?"

Riku had been thinking that.

"I still wonder why he came," Riku said. "His skills are coming in handy now, but a biochemical expert is an odd pick for a trip to find an object in space."

"Do you think they knew about the fungus, before?" Ardan asked.

Riku thought about it for a long moment, and then shook his head.

"Dr. Bernard seemed genuinely surprised by it on *Aurora Three*. I think he came for some other reason. I just wish I knew what it was."

"Me too, *mo chuisle*." Ardan pulled Riku closer to him and put his arm around him, anchoring him to his body. Weightlessness made cuddling more challenging than Riku would have expected. He did his best to snuggle into his lover's embrace and felt a dull longing for home.

"I think I'm over space flight," he said. Ardan laughed.

It wasn't much longer before the doctors brought the group together in the lounge space. They had put a projection of the princess up, complete with space suit and spore coating.

"This fungus, what exactly is it?" Ardan asked.

"Completely unlike anything we've seen before," Dr. Bernard said. "And it seems to have had a surprising effect on the princess's body—it has kept her alive."

"Well, isn't this exciting?" Declan said. "What is she? A zombie? The undead?"

"Frozen," Dr. Haider said. "Every cell in her body."

"Then how is she still alive?" Eural asked. "Doesn't she need food, water, air?"

"If she is frozen, the way we think she is, she wouldn't need any of those things. Her cells are not moving—so they aren't metabolizing. Her entire body is in a type of stasis."

"Can she be woken up?" Ardan asked.

"That's what we're not sure of," Dr. Bernard said. "But we think that maybe, if we can kill the fungus—without also hurting the princess—maybe she would just wake up, naturally."

"But we have to find a way to do that with what's on the ship," Ardan said, sighing.

"Why can't we take her back to L'Mondeau, figure it out there?" Eural asked.

"Because from what we can tell, the fungus feeds on oxygen. Not to breathe, the way we do. Actually feeds on it, using it to multiply and grow. If it somehow got out on L'Mondeau, it could overtake the planet."

The gathered faces looked appropriately somber at Dr. Bernard's declaration.

"How did it even get on the *Aurora Three*?" Riku asked.

"Unclear," Dr. Bernard said. "But possibly they encountered it on *Aurora One*, and somehow brought it back with them."

"Does the *Aurora One* have the same fungus on board?" Declan asked.

"Uncertain," Dr. Haider said. "There is something on the ship interfering with our scans."

"Is it the same thing messing with long distance communication?" Eural asked.

"Likely," Dr. Haider said. "But again, there is no way of knowing."

"So we go and have a look." Declan grinned at the group. "Who's up for another field trip?"

"With something there that is interfering with communications, a possibly-deadly fungus that may have originated there, and a mystery in airlock two still waiting to be solved?" Ardan shook his head. "I'm voting no."

"I believe there may be something on the *Prestige* that could kill the fungus," Dr. Bernard said.

"Doctor," Declan said quickly, staring hard at the older man. "A word."

Dr. Bernard scowled back, but nodded. The two moved away from the group, Riku's gaze heavy on them.

"Any idea what that's about?" Ardan asked Dr. Haider.

"Maybe," she said. She wouldn't elaborate.

Dr. Bernard and Declan came back then, Declan clearly upset by whatever conversation happened away from the others.

"Before your Queen approached us about this trip, we had intended to use the *Prestige* for another purpose," Declan said.

"We planned to experiment on Substance 248, the gas that The Thirteenth has been using, the same gas that was used in the attack on your princess Chavri on her naming day," Dr. Bernard said. "But we needed a safe, and secret place to do it."

"What is the nature of your experiments?" Dr. Haider asked.

Declan looked at Dr. Bernard, and nodded slightly. The doctor nodded back.

"Inoculation," he said. "We wanted to figure out if there was a way to create an inoculation to the poisonous effect of the gas. Moarga may take the brunt of the physical attacks from The Thirteenth, but Mehmtok gets more chemical warfare. We've had two suicide bombers in the past six months, both with this gas."

"And dozens died each time," Declan said.

"We never heard anything about that," Riku said.

"That's because our leaders thought it would be bad for business if word got out."

"And I, at least, was informed," Ardan said. "It was need to know," he offered to Riku along with an apologetic look.

"Why go to space for that? Surely there are better places in Mehmtok."

"Not where I can both keep my research secret, and have a measure of safety."

"The truth is," Declan said, "we're not sure who in Mehmtok can be trusted."

"The Thirteenth," Riku said.

"We think they've got support from some of the houses. There may even be spies in my house," Declan said. "On this ship are the only two Mehmtokians I know for sure I can trust."

"And you're trusting us with this?" Riku asked.

"I'm trusting Ardan and Dr. Haider," Declan responded. "And I suppose by extension, you and Eural. But only because I want something more than to keep this secret."

"The data on *Aurora One*," Ardan said.

"Which Dr. Bernard said may tell us more about this fungus and where it came from. Which suddenly has become very important. Tell them, doctor."

"I believe that something in the fungus could neutralize Substance 248, and potentially other poisonous gases as well. I have only started my research, but from the structure of the fungus, and how it reacts to oxygen and gives out nitrogen…"

"Yes," Dr. Haider said, nodding. "Yes, I can see that."

"And if that is the case, this strange fungus may be the key to neutralizing the most devastating weapon The Thirteenth uses."

"It could change everything," Ardan said, looking at Riku, who stared back in wonder.

"A space fungus?"

"The Aurora Fungus," Dr. Bernard said. "If I may suggest a name."

"Works for me," Ardan said.

"I would like to use Substance 248 on a portion of the samples we took. If my theory is sound, we could then use the gas to kill the spores covering Princess Chavri."

"The same gas that nearly killed her as an infant?" Riku shook his head. "This is crazy."

"I agree," Dr. Bernard said. "But crazy seems to be where we have landed. Declan has agreed to let me use the gas. I'll need Dr. Haider's help for the experiments."

"It's a sound theory," Dr. Haider said. "We'll test the samples, with your permission," she said, looking first at Ardan, then at Declan. It was unclear whose permission she thought she needed, but both men nodded.

The doctors quickly set up a test in the airlock, first feeding their spore sample a controlled amount of oxygen, and watching the spores transform into vine-like tendrils. Then they took a small amount of Substance 248, and injected it into the same air-tight container the new fungus was in. The effect was instantaneous, with the vines seeming to regress and shrink back to a spore state, and then the spores themselves seeming to implode and disappear. It was then that Dr. Haider noticed something particular—the container was filled with a higher concentration of oxygen than before. And more importantly, there was no trace of the gas left—the fungus seemed to absorb it all.

"It's a very promising result," Dr. Haider said to the others. "And if we had more time, I can think of an entire series of tests that I would like to follow up with. But we've taken as much time with this as we can. We need to decide—use the gas on the princess, or leave her here."

All eyes turned to Ardan. He rubbed the back of his scalp, and then sighed.

"We all thought she was dead. By rights, she should be, from natural causes if nothing else. We owe it to her to give her the best chance she can have to live."

"This is our best chance," Dr. Haider said gently. Ardan smiled back.

"Then please, doctor. Wake up my ancestor, will you?"

Chapter 20

Princess Chavri was strapped to the top of a storage crate just barely long enough to hold her body, which in turn was strapped to the floor of airlock two. After much discussion, it was decided that the best way to administer the gas to her was through her suit's air system. Dr. Haider had powered up the suit and was able to monitor the oxygen saturation rate through an external monitor. Dr. Bernard agreed to release the gas into her suit through a valve in the back in order to better control her exposure rate. No one knew how much she would need to kill the spores that had infected her. Both were in space suits to minimize risk of exposure to either the spores or the gas.

Eural and Geoff listened in from the bridge. Riku and Ardan waited just outside the airlock, ready to depressurize the airlock as a last resort to prevent the gas or the fungus from getting into the ship. Declan couldn't seem to decide where he wanted to be, and seemed to be floating all over, the space equivalent of pacing.

"Ready," Dr. Bernard said.

"Ready," Dr. Haider echoed. "Oxygen level is at zero percent."

Dr. Bernard turned the valve releasing Substance 248 into Chavri's suit.

"Saturation at three percent," he said.

Riku listened in on the com, wishing the process wouldn't take so long. By the time that saturation was reported to be at twenty-three percent, he realized he was tapping his hand against his thigh. At thirty-four percent, Ardan began to intentionally push himself up in order to bounce back down. At fifty-four percent, Chavri's oxygen rate began to go up.

"Start reducing the gas level," Dr. Haider ordered, and Dr. Bernard complied.

Ardan and Riku both braced themselves to stay still. Even Declan seemed impacted by the tension, gripping a cushion tightly in his hands.

"Oxygen at twenty percent," Dr. Haider said.

"Reducing Substance 248."

"Oxygen at thirty, thirty-four, thirty-nine, forty-four…"

"I'm going to turn off the gas. I think it's enough."

"Agreed," Dr. Haider said. "Oxygen over fifty."

Dr. Haider continued to read out the rates, and in a few minutes, she hit ninety percent.

"Stand by," she said.

Just then, a new noise could be heard on the coms system: coughing.

"She's waking up!" Dr. Haider exclaimed. "What's the Substance 248 level? Is there any trace left?"

"None," Dr. Bernard said.

Then the alarms in the suit started to go off.

Riku watched through the camera feed into the airlock as Chavri continued to cough and struggle, managing to get one arm free. She pulled at her helmet as though trying to tear it off.

"Hold her down!" Dr. Bernard yelled.

Dr. Haider tried to wrestle Chavri's hand away from her helmet.

"Get it off, get it off, get it off!" the princess was yelling. "Spores! Spores!" She got her other arm free and was trying to tear at her suit.

Dr. Haider was knocked back, and Dr. Bernard was struggling to hold Chavri's arms down. Making a choice, Dr. Haider twisted Chavri's helmet off before she could do damage to herself, and put her hands on Chavri's head, forcing her to look at her. It wasn't working. Dr. Haider then twisted her own helmet off and tried again, putting her face directly in front of the princess's so that she had no other place to look.

"You're safe!" she said. "The spores are gone. You're safe. Look at me. You're safe!"

"Gone?" Chavri asked.

"Gone," Dr. Haider said.

Chavri closed her eyes and took in deep breaths in a calming exercise that Riku recognized from his training.

Then her eyes shot open again, and she struggled to sit up.

"Stacia!" she shouted. "I have to get to her, I have to…" She struggled against her straps.

"Princess Chavri, will you be still!" Dr. Haider yelled. It had the desired effect and Chavri turned to stare at her. Then her eyes took in the sight of two helmet floating behind the doctor. Her hands flew to her mouth.

"Oh gods! My helmet!"

"No, it's all right. We can breathe this air," Dr. Haider said. "See? I'm breathing it."

Next to Riku, Ardan groaned. "No," he said. "What have we done?"

Riku couldn't understand. The princess was alive! She was awake and alive and Ardan should be celebrating. Princess Chavri, the lost princess of Moarga. Who was poisoned on her naming day....

Riku finally understood.

"She has an autoimmune disorder," he said into his coms. "She can't fight off infection! She needs her helmet."

Dr. Haider pressed her hand to her ear as though to steady her headpiece. Then she whipped out one of her many instruments and waved it over Chavri.

"Say again Riku," she asked.

"She has an autoimmune disorder," he said again. "She was poisoned on her naming day. Substance 248. She can't fight off any germs."

"Her scans are clear," Dr. Haider said.

"She is perfectly healthy," Dr. Bernard confirmed, scanning also.

Riku looked at Ardan, and Ardan shook his head. "Can you even detect autoimmune with those things?" Riku asked.

"Yes," Dr. Haider said with a touch of offense in her voice. "And I am reporting that her scans are clear. Whatever she had before—she's cured."

PART V:

Proclamations were issued, forbidding any approach to the castle, but these warnings were not needed, for within a quarter of an hour there grew up all around the park so vast a quantity of trees big and small, with interlacing brambles and thorns, that neither man nor beast could penetrate them.

Charles Perrault, The Sleeping Beauty in the Wood

Chapter 21

Ardan couldn't help but notice how often Chavri stared at his eyes, so like her father's, who he shared a name with. He knew that she had been struggling with the reality of her situation, with the idea that so much time had passed, and he wanted very much to comfort her. He just had no idea how.

There had been some debate about telling her anything at all, in letting her assume this was just a rescue mission and that everything was more or less the same back on L'Mondeau. But Chavri had immediately noticed the more modern scanners, had picked up on the subtle signifiers of rank, and had concluded, correctly, that both Ardan and Declan were royalty. Declan had been very pleased to be discovered, but Ardan had been worried. Chavri of course knew every royal in all the provinces—she was well trained and an excellent student. Their attempts at deception had fallen apart much quicker than anyone could have anticipated.

And then she got quiet. Processing, Ardan assumed. While technically she was his great great Aunt, Ardan had started to think of her as a niece. He had started to fuss over her, try to attend to her every potential need, until Riku and Dr. Haider told him to stop, Riku gently and Dr. Haider directly.

Now Chavri was camped out in front of a window that faced the *Aurora Three*, lost in thought.

"Exactly how will this work for Moarga?" Declan asked. "Technically she comes before even Queen Laney in the line of succession. Will the province suddenly be ruled by a twenty-year-old?"

Ardan thought that Declan was enjoying the situation way too much. From the look on his face, Riku obviously shared Ardan's opinion.

"We have a lot more to figure out before we think about that," he said.

Dr. Bernard came out from his lab in engineering, frowning down at a read out.

"Well, the good news is that your princess is in excellent condition," he said. "But I am still not sure we will have the same luck with the others."

"Why not?" Declan asked,

"Chavri had been exposed to Substance 248 before. What we know now and didn't know then is that it's more than just a poisonous gas. Something in it changes a person on the cellular level. Even the smallest exposure can have system-wide results. The others on the other ships—Chavri confirmed her crew had no prior exposure," Dr. Bernard continued. "We can assume the others didn't either, since use of Substance 248 didn't start until Chavri's father's reign."

"So we kill the fungus and bury the bodies. They've been assumed dead for centuries, and even if they lived out their natural lives, would still have been dead for centuries. I don't understand the issue," Declan said.

Ardan felt a strong urge to grab Declan's head and ram it up against the nearest bulkhead. It was Riku's turn to give him a look to remind him to calm down.

"They're people, MY people," he said. "And technically they

are still alive, and we are duty bound to do what we can to save them."

"Do we have any solutions, or just problems?" Declan snapped.

"I'm afraid we're stuck with where we started—we don't know what will happen when we expose the people in either ship to Substance 248. We have no way of knowing how much fungus there is, or how much gas to use. We know there will be an oxygen byproduct, but not how much, which poses its own issues due to oxygen's high flammability rate. We could be saving the people and the ships. We could be creating a disaster. We just don't know."

"So we start with *Aurora Three*," Chavri said, turning to face them. Ardan didn't think she'd been following along. "It's smaller, with fewer people. It should give us the best readings to make the *Aurora One* conversion go better. You have fire extinguishers—I saw them. It would be a simple matter to convert them so they shot out Substance 248 instead of fire retardant. That way we have a chance of controlling how much we let out."

Dr. Bernard stared at her, obviously both surprised and impressed.

"And the oxygen levels?"

"We monitor them," she said simply. "I think we aim to get the people in intact suits as soon as possible, and that way we can vent the air, if need be. I can do it from engineering, I know how."

"No, you'll tell someone," Ardan said, pushing himself forward to look Chavri in the eye. "As much as you are concerned about your crew, you won't be there."

"Why not?" she asked. "I'm expendable. I'm not even really supposed to be alive—I'm out of my time. If something happens to me, it won't actually matter."

"You're the heir," Riku said automatically.

Chavri visibly recoiled from the statement.

"Not anymore," she said. "My time has passed. Prince Ardan is the heir. I'm just an extra body you guys picked up on your mission. I am the very definition of expendable."

"You're not," Ardan said gently. He wanted to put an arm around her, make some physical contact that could be comforting. "Not to me."

Chavri looked into his eyes, and after a moment, turned away.

"You have his eyes," she said. "And I'm sure you're very nice. Likeable. Probably even lovable. But what you have told me is that everyone I have ever known or loved is gone. Everyone, except for the two souls on *Aurora Three*. They are all I have left. I will do anything, *anything*, to save them. Do you understand? I have to save them. I have to."

She closed her eyes again and engaged in a calming exercise, one well practiced. Ardan was impressed by how quickly she was able to tamper down what was obviously very strong emotion.

"Beyond that, if you're going to tell me I can't go because I'm the heir, then I will tell you that technically that means I out-rank you, having been born very much before you, and that means that I am no longer asking for permission—I'm giving orders. I'm going. And you better not try to stop me."

Ardan was impressed, and by the look on Riku's face, his guard was too.

"I'll go with her," he said. "The two of us. I'll make sure she's safe." Riku looked up at him and smiled. "It's a Dvorak tradition."

"I was wondering about that. You look so much like Riska."

"He was my great great grandfather," he said.

"That makes Stacia your relative—he was her uncle." Chavri hoped that would help make this as personal for Riku as it was for her.

He paused, clearly thinking.

"Great great Aunt Eva's daughter," he said, and Chavri nodded. "I won't let anything happen to Stacia. Or to you."

"Wonderful," Declan said, clapping his hands together. "Let's tell the others and get started on that fire extinguisher conversion."

Ardan wanted to protest, but Declan was already moving, patting him on the shoulder as he passed. "We have a plan," Declan said. "Let's just get it over with so that we can go home. Ship intact." Dr. Bernard followed him back to engineering, leaving Ardan with Riku and Chavri.

"I have no intention of losing you two," Ardan said. "So take every precaution. No risks."

"Be careful," Chavri said. "The unofficial Moargan motto. Trust me, I know it well."

Ardan laughed. He bet she did know it well. He wondered what her life might have been like. He'd heard stories—always in a mask of one kind or another, never able to touch another person. He had noticed that she had a tendency to keep physical distance between herself and others, an old habit he was sure. And a sad habit. Again, he wanted to hug her, pat her on the hand, make some contact.

"You will go over the schematics of the *Aurora Three* with Riku. Tell him all the things he doesn't already know, the inside information. Use the projection, map out as much of the fungus as you can remember."

"Oh, I remember it all," Chavri said. "It may have been hundreds of years ago for you two, but for me, it was only hours ago. Don't worry, we got this." She turned and pushed off from her couch, stealing one last look at the *Aurora Three* through the window. "See you soon," he heard her whisper.

Chapter 22

Chavri pulled her helmet down over her head and twisted it to seal it in place. As she heard the familiar hiss of air pumping into her suit, she felt tension she wasn't even aware of holding release. As happy as she had been to hear that she was cured of the condition that plagued her entire life, she also had been having a hard time accepting the new rules. Floating around an unprotected space all willy nilly, no need to ensure every inch of it had been disinfected. Breathing the same air as other people. Not wearing anything over her face, and no one around her wearing anything on theirs. It was everything she always wanted, but also everything she had always been taught to fear.

The first time Dr. Haider brushed her arm while taking blood from her, Chavri jumped. Even though the doctor was wearing gloves, Chavri still felt that touch like a burn. It had been years since any person had taken her blood. And before that they had been wearing containment suits that very much resembled the space suit Chavri was putting on. This was one of the suits from the *Prestige*, a modern and slicker design. It was a universal size, but with a press of a button, extra material around the elbows, wrists, ankles, and knees retracted so that the suit became Chavri sized. Various pockets and pouches could be put on or removed, making the suit highly customizable. Chavri wondered why suit technology would improve, considering how rare space travel had become. But then Riku had told her about the biochemical attacks that had become more and more frequent—the containment suits used were essentially space suits worn planet-side. Chavri was greatly disturbed by this news. Still, putting on the suit gave Chavri a sense of coming home.

It was quick work to load up her other gear, including a wrench and a few other tools. The last thing she put on was a bag holding an extra space suit, a suit repair kit for Stacia's suit, and a helmet for Lysa.

At last, she was ready to go. Riku had the newly-altered fire extinguisher-turned-gas-tank strapped to his back with a reserve tank of Substance 248. He appeared to be ready as well, and gave her a thumbs up to signal so.

"Coms check," she heard Ardan say through the speakers in her helmet.

"Loud and clear," Riku said.

"Good here," Chavri added.

"Depressurizing airlock," Riku said, and went to a panel next to the inner door. Chavri was impressed by the tech. The *Prestige* had been retrofitted over the last centuries, and there were lots of little differences that Chavri noticed, including updated panels and consoles.

Riku motioned Chavri over toward the outer door, and she complied.

"Feel ready for this?" he asked.

"Definitely," Chavri said.

The airlock finished depressurizing much sooner than Chavri was expecting. At least that upgrade felt useful. Chavri took a firm hold on a nearby handle, and Riku opened the door. Riku motioned up and Chavri saw a rope stretching between the two ships.

"How we got you," he said. He clipped a line from his belt to the rope, and Chavri pulled one from her belt and did the same. Riku went first, easily pulling himself along to the opposite ship. Chavri waited until he was safely on the other side, then started her own trek. As she made it over, Riku reached out a hand to help pull her in the last few centimeters. Riku twisted open the airlock and they both went inside.

Chavri didn't like how dark it was. When the *Aurora Three* was running, this room was bathed in light, a view screen showing what was on the other side of the door, just as one there showed what was in the airlock in lieu of windows. It had seemed like a fine system at the time, but now seemed pointless. It was a much longer wait for the airlock to pressurize than on the *Prestige*.

"Brace yourself," Riku said. "As soon as I open the door, hyphae—which look like vines—will start to grow into the airlock. They'll take all the oxygen, and then stop growing. Once they do, we'll be able to get inside, and get to the crew, understand? I want to secure them first, before we try any of this." He patted the tank on his back. "You ready?"

"Yes," Chavri said. She grabbed a handle by the door to anchor herself there.

"*Prestige*, we are opening the inner door of the airlock," Riku announced.

"Roger," Ardan said. "Good luck."

Riku turned the wheel and pulled the door open.

Immediately hyphae started growing into the airlock area. Chavri pulled as much of her body away from it as she could, revulsion and fear thick in her throat.

"It will only get so long, and then stop," Riku said. "Scan for oxygen levels."

Chavri pushed buttons on her wrist pad until she could see a display of oxygen levels in the room. The hyphae grew as the levels dropped, and once they hit zero, the hyphae became still.

"I think that's what Lysa was trying to tell me, before," she said to Riku. "She'd figured most of it out. But then the spores got her."

"Away team, status?"

"Oxygen levels at zero. The hypha has halted its growth. We're going after the crew now." Riku turned and smiled at Chavri. "We'll get them," Riku said.

He pulled himself through the doorway, careful to avoid any of the vine-like growths of the fungus. Chavri trailed after him, lighting her way with the flashlight attached to her wrist. When she saw the mass of hyphae surrounding Stacia's body, she let out an involuntary whimper.

"How can we get her out of all of that?" she asked.

"We'll use the gas," Riku said, though he sounded uncertain. "Let's get Lysa first. She's easier." He shone his light to where the older woman was floating. Her shirt had snagged a vine, keeping her in place. She looked like a perfectly preserved body washed in orange spores, her eyes frozen open. Chavri had to choke back a sob.

"It's going to be all right," Riku said. "You came back. They will, too."

Chavri had a lot of doubts. But she kept her light steady as

Riku made his way toward Lysa's body, carefully pushing hyphae away with a long metal rod. It was easier to push Lysa back from the hypha than pull the hypha off from her, but it was still hard for Chavri to watch Lysa's body be moved like a side of beef. Once he got her free from the hypha, Riku was able to move it away and get a rope on Lysa, attached to her belt. He was extra careful on his way back to Chavri, and Chavri helped pull Lysa back into the airlock, securing her to the wall with the same rope. She tried not to look at Lysa's face too much so that she wouldn't break down into tears.

"*Prestige*, we've secured the pilot in the airlock."

Chavri pulled the extra suit out of her bag and began to wrestle Lysa's stiff body into it. Riku helped as best he could. Chavri pulled the helmet off the chain on her back and secured it on to Lysa.

"We can take her back now," she said. "When we're ready."

Riku patted her on the shoulder. "Ready for Stacia?" Chavri nodded and Riku pulled the tank of Substance 248 from his back. "*Prestige*, we are going to distribute the gas."

"Roger, away team," Ardan said through the coms. If the prince was nervous, he kept it from his voice.

Riku pulled the hose out and then anchored his feet under handles near the entrance of the airlock. Chavri braced herself against the side of the airlock, wrapping her legs on either side of the door frame and holding a handle above her head with one hand while grabbing hold of the back of Riku's suit with the other. Once Riku turned on the extinguisher, the force of the gas going one way would to push him back the other.

"Ready," she said.

Riku squeezed the discharge lever, and immediately started to float back. It took all of Chavri's strength to keep him in place as he struggled to point the hose toward the mass of hyphae surrounding Stacia's body.

The gas was absorbed by the fungus, and it looked like their plan was working as the hyphae immediately around Stacia began to shrink. But then something strange happened. The hyphae closest to Riku began to move as though avoiding the gas, snaking around to either side of his spray. Chavri couldn't be sure she was seeing what she thought she was seeing as her flashlight wasn't pointed in the right direction. It took her too long to realize that the moving hyphae were hugging the walls of engineering and growing toward Riku until the sharp point of one thrust into his thigh.

Shocked by the pain, Riku released the lever on the extinguisher and reached down to his leg. A spike on the vine impaled his hand, and on instinct, he dropped the hose as well, the extinguisher floating away from him. Chavri yanked on his suit, trying to pull him away from the hypha and into the airlock, but he was stuck.

"Riku, get your leg free!" she shouted.

"Chavri," he said. "Chavri, my leg is numb, and my hand. I think my suit's been compromised. Chavri, you need to…"

Then she heard the sound of coughing, and then nothing at all. Chavri disentangled herself from the doorway and pulled herself into the airlock. Riku's body seemed stuck in place, his limbs as frozen as Lysa's.

"Away team, status!" Ardan shouted. But Chavri felt as frozen as Riku was. She closed her eyes and focused on her breathing. "Riku, Chavri, what the hell is happening?"

Chavri counted down from ten, focusing on her breathing. Her suit was beeping. Riku was frozen. She was alone on the *Aurora Three*, again. Four, three, two...

"Riku!" Ardan shouted again.

"He's alive," Chavri said. "But his suit was compromised. Like mine. He...he's frozen. Spores got into the suit." She took another deep breath. "The gas caused a strange reaction. The hyphae, they...moved."

"What do you mean?" Chavri recognized Dr. Bernard's voice. She stared at Riku, and then shone her light past him the best she could to see the extinguisher full of Substance 248 floating roughly between Riku and Stacia. Riku had succeeded in one thing—Stacia was no longer covered in hyphae.

"They reacted to the gas. They moved away from it," Chavri said. "Toward the airlock. Toward the most recent source of oxygen." She was thinking hard, trying to figure out her next steps.

"We're sending someone to you," Ardan said.

"You can't," Chavri said. "Riku, he was in the doorway of the airlock when...when he was frozen. He's blocking the door. I have to move him. And first I have to get the hypha out of his leg and hand. And out of the doorway. Gods—they're everywhere."

She could feel panic climbing up her throat, tightening everything, making it harder for her to breathe.

"Chavri," Ardan said, his voice sounding surprisingly like her father's. "Chavri, you can do this. I'll talk you through it." Chavri nodded though there was no one there to see her. "First, I need you to get the extinguisher. Can you do that?"

"Yes," Chavri said. "I have to get by Riku, but I think I can."

She took out her wrench, meager protection though it was, and pushed herself away from the airlock wall and toward the entryway. She snagged the top of the doorway with her hand, using the wrench to gently push the hypha closest to her away. It pushed back easily, and Chavri took a breath of relief.

"Does fungus do that?" she asked. "Move away from danger-ous things?"

"They can respond to stimuli, but they can't actually move," Dr. Bernard said. "I suspect that what happened was that as the gas was absorbed by the fungus and released oxygen, that oxygen caused new hyphae to grow."

"It really looked like it moved," Chavri said. "There is more on the inner walls, and it grew toward Riku, and he had the ex-tinguisher."

"And the gas made the fungus produce more oxygen. I assure you, the fungus didn't seek him out. It doesn't have that sort of intelligence."

Chavri wasn't convinced.

"Fungus on L'Mondeau doesn't," she said. She eyed the vine-like structures warily as she made her way to the extinguisher. She snagged it and hooked the hose over her arm as she worked her way back to the airlock, eyes darting around for any sign that the fungus was aware of her actions and responding to them.

"I'm back in the airlock," she said. "I have the extinguisher."

"Good, now you're going to spray the area around Riku, get

the hypha attached to him to retreat."

Chavri didn't like that idea. For one, using the extinguisher was going to push her backward, and it was going to be hard to brace against that. For another, regardless of what reason Dr. Bernard came up with, she knew the hyphae grew toward Riku, toward the source of the gas that was basically killing the fungus.

Chavri could only think of one way to brace herself and spray at the hyphae that trapped Riku. She hooked her arm around his, which was stiff and frozen, his hand still on the spike. Chavri used a short retractable rope to connect herself to the opposite handle, locking the rope in place. Then she aimed the hose and squeezed the lever slowly, hoping to let only a little gas out of the high-pressure tank.

The force was greater than Chavri was anticipating, and she almost lost her grip on the extinguisher as she felt herself propelled backwards. Between the rope and Riku's body, she managed to stay in place and wrestled the hose back into position. The hypha immediately began to shrink, the spike sliding out of Riku's hand and the end of the hypha pulling out of his thigh. Chavri released the lever and pushed the tank into the airlock, whirling around with her flashlight to catch any additional hyphae growing in her direction. She could swear that many were a lot closer than they were before, sharp ends all pointing her way. But for the moment they were still.

Chavri grabbed the bottom rails where Riku had jammed his feet and one by one pushed them loose, making his body float into the airlock where it gently bumped into Lysa's and ricocheted off. She turned to make sure all the hyphae stayed where they were, and then went into the airlock to secure Riku's body.

"I have Riku free and in the airlock," she said.

"Try to repair his suit so that we can get him back here," Ardan said.

Chavri pulled the repair kit from her bag, using a specialized scanning tool to find and detect holes. Fortunately, it was just the two obvious ones, and the patch material went on easily, the same tool being used to activate a compound in the patches to make them adhere to the suit with airtight seals. The glove was slightly harder, since it had holes on both sides. Chavri felt like she should also try to treat Riku's hand, but the blood was frozen solid like little red icicles tinged orange by the spores.

Most improbably of all though was that Chavri was still getting life signs from Riku. He wasn't breathing, and he wasn't moving, and there was no cellular movement of any kind. But somehow her scanners still read him as alive.

"The suit is repaired," she said. "He's going to need medical attention when he…wakes up." She put the repair kit in his pocket to secure it since she knew Riku wasn't going anywhere.

"Now you're going to cut the hyphae and get the door closed. Eural and Dr. Bernard will come to you. They'll get Lysa and Riku back to the *Prestige*, and then get Stacia," he said. "You're coming back to the *Prestige* too. You've done enough."

Chavri wanted to protest but there was no point now, not when there were still several steps between her and that inevitability. She searched her equipment for a knife, and then searched Riku's. The only place left was his pockets. Chavri felt awkward reaching around his frozen limbs, but found a large folding knife.

She unfolded it and looked at the hyphae in the door. There were three particularly large and thick ones coming in from the sides and over what Chavri thought of as the floor—up and down were relative in space. There were also two smaller tendrils reaching around the door frame higher up, each about as thick as a carrot. Chavri decided to start with those. She was anxious about trying to cut anything, still mostly convinced the fungus was going to fight back.

Chavri pulled herself to the doorway and used a pair of pliers to hold the hypha tendril still. As she sliced the knife down into the fungus, her eyes darted up and around, looking for some sort of movement among the other hyphae.

The knife slipped off the surface of the hypha. Confused, Chavri cut down again, and again, the knife slid sideways. It was like trying to cut a carrot which had suddenly developed a thin metal plating. Chavri tried the other side of the hypha, and again, the knife couldn't penetrate. She tried to make cuts on other parts of the hypha, but they also resisted. She tried to use the pliers to bend the hypha, and it wouldn't bend.

Chavri moved to the other hyphae in the doorway, and all her attempts to cut them were unsuccessful. She thought about trying to go into engineering and cut them off from the source, but even trying to trace the path of these particular hyphae was going to be incredibly difficult. Chavri had the strong suspicion that those too would be impossible to cut.

"Um, *Prestige*?" she said. "We have a problem."

"What's going on, Chavri?"

"I can't cut the hyphae," she said. "The outer skin has hardened. It is too hard for the blade to cut through—and something about it also makes the blade slide off when I try to exert force. All the hyphae are exhibiting this trait."

"Impossible," Dr. Bernard said. "We cut through one quite easily when we were there. Try again."

"You only had one to cut through?" Chavri asked. The scientist part of her brain was adding up the evidence and concluding that the fungus was definitely putting up some sort of defense. She shuddered to think about it. She wondered now if the spores were part of its defense mechanism—freeze your attackers and they can't hurt you. As an added bonus, once a spore was exposed to enough oxygen and room, it would sprout. "There are three large hyphae and two smaller ones blocking the door. There is no way for me to cut through them."

"Again, that is impossible," Dr. Bernard said.

"And it's impossible that a princess from your great great grandfather's day could be frozen and resuscitated. Oh wait, that happened, too."

Chavri's fear was getting to her, and the strain of trying to watch all the hyphae around her was making her irritable.

"Chavri, it's Dr. Haider. We're still going to solve this. You're going to use the gas on the hyphae in the doorway. Can you do that?"

"Doctor, they grow when I use it. The ones in the immediate area shrink away, but other ones grow—toward the source of the gas. I've seen it twice now." As Chavri said it, a thought began to occur to her. "They grow from the ends of the hyphae, right? They don't move so much as grow in a certain direction. What if

I wedge the extinguisher somewhere else? Off to the side maybe. Then maybe the hyphae will grow toward it." What she didn't add but thought was, *and away from me.*

"So long as the hyphae in the doorway shrink back enough for you to close the door, I don't see why not," Dr. Haider said. Her voice held a lot of patience and a slight tone of humoring. Chavri didn't care if everyone else thought she was crazy—she knew what she was seeing.

"On it," she said. She took the extinguisher and carefully floated through the doorway, watching for any spikes or errant hyphae. She found a spot relatively free of the vines near where the controls for the electrical system on the ship were. Frustrated by the dark all around her, she opened the panel and flipped all the switches that would reset the electrical systems in the ship, hoping but not expecting them to turn on. To her surprise, the panel came to life, and lights turned on throughout engineering. They were the emergency lights, and cast a reddish glow over everything, which made the orange spores look like flecks of dried blood covering every surface.

She could see better, but she didn't like what she saw.

"Chavri?" Ardan asked.

"I was able to reset the power on the ship," she said. "We have emergency power." She checked the meters. "Not a lot, maybe another hour's worth before the energy drains completely. But something."

"Very good!"

Chavri wished that she could feel pleased with herself, but was way too tense for that. With greater visibility, she was able to get the extinguisher in place without much effort, jamming the hose through a handle to keep it mostly pointed at the airlock doorway. The hard part was finding a way to get the lever to stay open. She sacrificed her pliers for the task, and then pulled herself away as quickly as possible.

The green gas looked blackish under the red light, like smoke blowing out over the hyphae. Everywhere the gas touched, the hyphae retreated, shrinking into themselves. At the same time, other hyphae started growing, as if to compensate. And they all started growing toward the extinguisher.

Some had made their way behind the extinguisher, the ends pushing it loose from where Chavri had wedged it. It separated from its hose, the pliers keeping the valve open and the force of the pressurized gas launching it zooming around engineering like a rocket, blanketing everything with Substance 248. The hyphae moved all around Chavri in response, and she struggled to keep them at bay with her wrench. Only one puncture of her suit, and this would be all over, and she, Lysa, Riku, and Stacia would be lost forever, with no way for anyone to get to them.

That's when Chavri saw it—Stacia's body was now free floating and no longer tangled up in hyphae. The gas, floating in thick rolling clouds throughout the space, had gotten to her, too. Taking her chance, Chavri launched herself at Stacia, colliding with her body and using an overhead handle to halt her momentum. With her other hand, she grabbed Stacia's arm and pulled her close, using the retractable wire on her belt to attach her body to Chavri's. Then Chavri moved as quickly as possible toward the airlock.

But instead of moving away from the door, the hyphae around it had increased, grown thicker, crossing over the open area. There was no way for Chavri to get through. Panicked, she looked around. There was a clear spot near the control panel, and she pulled herself and Stacia toward it, working hard to free Stacia's body from several hyphae that tried to snag her. Chavri got Stacia's body behind her, closer to the panel, and turned around, finally taking in all of engineering.

The extinguisher was spinning in the middle of the room spraying out Substance 248, and hyphae were in turns shrinking away from the gas and trying to grow toward the extinguisher in a terrifying dance.

"*Prestige*, it's all gone wrong," she said. "The tank is loose, and the hyphae have blocked the door to the airlock. And I swear by the gods, Dr. Bernard, if you say that's impossible, I will scream."

"Chavri," Dr. Haider said. "The power is on—can you vent the air from engineering? All of it?"

"I think so," Chavri said. She turned to the panel. "I'll have to reroute the system through here."

"Do it!"

Chavri worked quickly trying to focus on everything she knew about the *Aurora Three's* electrical system. Stacia had been much better at this stuff than she was. Finally, she figured out which cable to put where. She flipped the switch.

Nothing happened.

"It's not working," she said.

"Chavri, you've got to vent the cabin."

Chavri put her hands to her helmet and tried to think.

"The second airlock," she said. "We closed it off because of the damage. If I can get to it, I can open it."

"Go," Dr. Haider said. Chavri turned and searched for a way to secure Stacia to the wall and away from the hyphae. She only had one thing on her that would work—the retractable wire. She unclipped it from her belt and clipped one side to one handle, then wound it around Stacia's belt and clipped the other to another handle, effectively strapping Stacia in place.

Then Chavri looked out over engineering. She needed to get to the other side, past the spinning extinguisher, through the clouds of smoke-like gas, and through wildly waving hyphae and all their spikes. She looked up. The hyphae had coated electrical equipment and were mostly on the sides of engineering. The extinguisher was spinning near the top center of engineering. Her best bet was to float up near the relative top of the room, go through the cloud of smoke, and out the other side.

Chavri took a deep breath and pulled herself up, finding handles to propel herself along and keeping her body as parallel to what she was thinking of as the ceiling as possible. The clouds of smoke were thick and all encompassing; her wrist reflected light off the cloud like it was a bank of fog. Chavri caught something in her peripheral and barely saw the hypha in time to avoid its rapier tip. But avoiding it pushed her off course, and in the midst of the gas, she lost any sense of which direction was which. She pulled her wrist pad closer to her helmet, trying to see the readout in all the gas. Another hypha was coming at her from her left, and she shoved forward, hoping she was going in the right direction, desperate to avoid it.

Eventually she broke through the gas-cloud. She was near enough to the airlock, and soon was able to pull herself down to the panel next to the door. The hyphae were thinner here, but to work on the panel she would have to turn her back to the mass of movement behind her. She hated the idea and twisted herself the best she could to try to see as much as possible.

"I'm at the airlock door," she said quietly, feeling the need to whisper. She used a small drill to unscrew the panel. It was a matter of programming in the override on the lock, and then she would be able to get the door open manually.

It took several moments longer than Chavri wanted it to. She caught movement above her, and ducked to avoid a hypha, its long spikes scraping against the top of her helmet. Chavri kept her head low as she reached blindly for the handle of the airlock. She shoved her wrench in her pocket and used both hands to turn the wheel. Alarm bells went off telling her that the airlock behind was not sealed. She ignored them all and shoved the door open.

Immediately, air was sucked out of the *Aurora Three*. Chavri barely managed to keep hold of the wheel. The pressure was such that hyphae were being sucked out as well, and since the fungus was all one organism, where one hypha went, the others followed. A clump of hyphae smacked Chavri square on, and she lost her grip, her hands scrambling for anything she could possibly hold on to. The airlock had been damaged, the outer door torn and bent by the impact the ship had made against an asteroid so many years ago, but there was still some structure there. Chavri was slammed against what was left of the far wall of the airlock. The fungus had clogged the hole in the hull, but without atmosphere was rapidly withering, losing mass. Chavri wrapped her arm around a handle and hugged it as tight as she could. She could tell pressure was building again, and with a whoosh of air, the fungus was pulled out of its hole, tearing off pieces of ship with it as it was sucked out into the vacuum of space.

The section of the hull Chavri clung to bent and buckled, and she was knocked loose, one hand snagging the handle while her body was whipped around, the last of the air from the *Aurora Three* rushing past her. Her fingers lost their grip and she flew backwards, flailing, arms and legs reaching for any purchase.

Her back thudded against the edge of the hull, flipping her around, and she saw loose wire dangling in front of her. She reached for it, but it slid through her hands.

Every alarm in her suit was blaring, and Chavri could just make out Ardan's voice shouting through her coms. The sound cut through her panic, and she focused on the wire.

Grab it, she told herself. *Just grab the wire. Everything will be all right if you just. Grab. The. Wire.*

Finally, her hand caught, and as quickly as she could, she wrapped the wire around her wrist. She was out of wire in front of her and still moving fast. Her body jerked at the end like a balloon on a string, the force causing her to ricochet back toward the hull of the *Aurora Three*. With her other hand she reached out for any purchase, finally finding one of the external handles. She gripped it with all her strength, halting her momentum, and focused on bringing her body as close to the hull as possible.

She was still, at last.

"Chavri!" Ardan was yelling.

"Here," she said, exhaustion and adrenaline making her voice shake. "I'm here."

"Chavri, you have to get to Stacia. Her suit isn't sealed. You didn't get to fix it."

Chavri could hear alarm bells coming through the coms.

"Ardan?" she asked.

"The explosion knocked the *Aurora Three* toward the *Prestige*. The ships are still connected. Eural and Geoff are on it. Get to Stacia."

Fear induced strength surged through her limbs. Chavri looked up and got her bearings. She wasn't far from the hole in the hull. She pulled herself along the surface of the ship, using handles and protruding equipment, until she got to the edge. She swung her legs over, twisting and going feet-first inside. Once inside where the airlock used to be, it was easier to find things to grab on to. Just as she got to the inner door, the ship tilted hard to the left, knocking her off the handle she'd been holding. She pushed her legs down, felt them sliding across the wall of the airlock until they pressed against something. She grabbed a handle and held on as the ship twisted back the other direction under her. Being more careful with her grip, she continued her trek through the door, and then braced herself in the doorway while yanking the door closed.

There was still no atmosphere in engineering, but as far as Chavri could see in the red emergency lights, there was no fungus anymore either. Chavri twisted the door shut to seal it, and then launched herself across the room. The room was in complete disarray, the force of air being sucked into space having ripped several panels off, and Chavri felt fear gnawing at her spine, terrified that Stacia wouldn't be where she left her.

But she was, still strapped in, limbs still frozen. Chavri unhooked her as quickly as possible, using the retractable wire to connect Stacia's body to her own, and then propelled herself to the other airlock, the door now clear of hyphae. She landed hard against the edge, Stacia's body bouncing off her. But she held firm, and then yanked the wire and pulled Stacia into the airlock. She got inside and shoved the door closed, twisted the wheel, and then launched herself at the panel next to it to pressurize the cabin, praying there was still air, that the system was still working.

She turned the handle. Immediately the panel lit up and told her that pressurization was in progress.

Chavri turned to Stacia, pulling her body around to look inside her helmet. Her face appeared normal with no sign of ebullism, free from burst blood vessels. And free from spores as well. But as Chavri watched, a light orange dusting around her nose and mouth began to grow bigger. In horror, she realized that the spores that Stacia had inhaled were still in her body, and starting to take over her face. In time they would fill up her suit again, and when they reached the hole in her suit, they would sprout out and take over the airlock that was even now filling with oxygenated air.

Chavri launched herself at Riku, pulling the suit repair kit from his pocket. As she got back to Stacia, she could see that her face was completely coated in spores again, and they were traveling down her neck. Chavri fumbled with the repair kit in her panic, but got a patch out, slapping it down on the material and using the tool to activate the compound that would seal it in place. Once she was sure it was sealed, she scanned all over Stacia's body to confirm that the only rupture to her suit was in her hip. It took a second to recalibrate the scan to account for the fact that Stacia's suit was a different type than Riku's and there was no onboard system to connect to. But eventually the readout confirmed: suit integrity intact. Chavri followed this up with a visual confirmation, rotating Stacia's body and running her flashlight over every patch of suit she could to look for any sign of spores.

She could see none.

"Chavri, Chavri come in," Ardan said. "We've got the ships stabilized. What's your status?"

"I have her," Chavri said. "I have all of them." She pulled Stacia's body closer to her own. "I won't let you go," she whispered to Stacia.

Chapter 28

The make-shift lab in the airlock on the *Prestige* was crowded. Dr. Bernard had his tank of Substance 248, Dr. Haider had her scanning equipment, and Chavri had three bodies strapped in various places in the airlock. The one on the makeshift table in the middle was Riku's. Chavri would have preferred they started with Stacia, but she also understood the fear that Ardan was feeling when he said that Riku would go first.

Everyone was concerned about Riku's wounds and the doctors had no idea what would happen with spores or Substance 248 getting into his bloodstream.

"Ready," Dr. Haider said.

"Proceeding," Dr. Bernard stated. He turned on the tank for Substance 248, and started reporting out the numbers. Eventually, the spore count went down, and the oxygen level went up, and then it was time to turn off the Substance 248 tank, and then the oxygen level was maxed, and then Riku was coughing.

"All the spores are gone," Dr. Bernard reported. With that, Dr. Haider helped Riku off with his helmet and started pulling his suit off him, starting with his gloves. His blood was flowing then, but the doctors had to get to the wounds. Chavri watched as a droplet of blood floated across her view.

"Got the hand covered in bandage," Dr. Bernard said. Dr. Haider was still pulling Riku's suit off. He seemed disoriented, but compliant.

"You're safe," Chavri said. It had helped her when she was

told that, and she hoped it helped Riku too. It took a second for his eyes to focus on her, and she repeated herself. "You're safe. I'm here with you. You're not alone."

He nodded.

Dr. Haider had gotten his suit off and cut away the fabric from the thin leggings he was wearing underneath. Dr. Bernard covered the wound in Riku's thigh while droplets of blood continued to float away from it.

"The wound needs to be closed," he said. Dr. Haider came around to his side and took out the stitching instrument, using a type of bioengineered glue to seal the wound with something flesh-like that would fall off when the skin underneath healed. It had the side effect of generally preventing scars.

"How do you feel?" Dr. Haider asked.

"Glad to be alive—and not covered in spores anymore." Riku smiled at the doctor, and then looked past him at Chavri.

"I was supposed to save you," he said.

"It was my turn to save a Dvorak," she replied, smiling at him.

Once they got Riku situated on the side of the room next to Chavri, the doctors started to strap Stacia to their makeshift operating bench.

Riku couldn't go inside the ship because they didn't want to risk contamination until everyone was spore-free. Chavri felt weird being in a suit while Riku wasn't, so she twisted off her helmet, and attached it to the wall so that it wouldn't float away. Then she undid her gloves, one at a time.

"Do you hate wearing those things as much as I do?" Riku

asked her.

"I spent most of my life in one or another, or else locked away in a hermetically sealed room. I guess you can say I'm used to it."

"Yeah, but do you hate it?"

Chavri considered his question for a moment.

"Yes, I do. I really do."

He motioned for her to turn around, and as she did, he undid the attachments in the back, letting her wriggle her way out of the suit. Then she was free, unencumbered, her skin and lungs and everything sharing the same air as Riku.

"Better?" he asked.

"Yes," she said. She turned her focus back to Stacia, who the doctors were prepping for the procedure. "She's going to be so shocked to see me like this," she said. "Do you know I've never actually been able to touch her? Not without gloves or suits or helmets between us. When we were little, we played together on opposite sides of a force field. We've never shared the same air."

"That sounds horrible," Riku said.

"Yes. She needs to wake up," she said quietly. "She needs to be all right. She'll be all right and I'll get to hug her, really hug her. But first, she has to wake up."

She felt Riku's hand take hers, and squeeze it, and felt some small measure of comfort. His skin was warm, palms calloused. It was the first hand she had ever remembered touching, and she instantly thought about what it would be like to hold Stacia's hand like this.

Chavri watched intently as the doctors completed their tasks, getting all the tanks in place and making sure Stacia was securely locked down.

"Ready," Dr. Haider said.

"Proceeding," Dr. Bernard said.

The next few minutes were the longest of Chavri's life. She didn't realize you could be so aware of the sound of your own breath without wearing a helmet. The sound of the doctors' voices felt like they were coming from another room. Only the pressure from Riku's hand kept her grounded, kept her from screaming, kept her from crying.

"All the spores are gone," Dr. Bernard said. There was something in his voice, some hesitation.

"What's wrong?" she asked.

"Oxygen levels at max," Dr. Haider said. She moved forward and took Stacia's helmet off.

"She's not coughing," Chavri realized.

"She's arrhythmic," Dr. Bernard announced.

"Get her suit off, we need to try chest compressions," Dr. Haider said. Chavri pushed forward and started pulling the material off of Stacia. When she had it down to Stacia's waist, Dr. Haider started cutting the shirt off her.

"You need to tilt her head back, pinch her nose closed, and then breathe into her mouth," Dr. Haider said. Chavri had seen vids of the procedure and did as she was asked.

"Starting compressions," Dr. Haider said. She counted them out, and when she got to the end of her count, instructed Chavri to breathe again. Two breaths, and then more compressions.

"Come on Stacia!" Chavri begged.

Just then, Stacia's hand came up and she pushed at Dr. Haider's hands.

"Heart rate normal," Dr. Bernard said.

Chavri put her hand on Stacia's face.

"I've got you," she said. "I'm here. You're all right."

Stacia touched Chavri's hand, and then reached out to touch her face.

"You're not wearing your helmet," she said, her eyes widening in fear.

"It's fine," Chavri said, smiling. "I don't need it."

"You don't?" Stacia asked, still confused. Chavri held Stacia's hand to her cheek. She realized then that she was crying, had been crying.

"I'm cured," she said. "Everything is going to be better." She pressed her forehead against Stacia's. "Just don't ever die on me, understand?"

"Whatever you say, my princess," Stacia said. Chavri laughed.

Chapter 24

Stacia, Lysa, and Chavri were huddled together in one cabin. It was a cramped fit, but it was also the only place where they had any modicum of privacy.

"Centuries," Lysa said, shaking her head. "I still can't wrap my mind around it. It doesn't feel real."

"I keep thinking that we'll go back to L'Mondeau and everything will be the way we left it. And then I look at Ardan, or Riku, and I remember," Chavri said. She had her arm around Stacia's shoulder, still relishing the skin-to-skin contact. She hadn't left Stacia's side since Stacia woke up, and used every excuse she could to make contact. It seemed that Stacia was more than fine with this, and often Chavri reached for Stacia's hand to find the other already reaching for hers.

They hadn't talked about it. They hadn't had time or space to talk about it. But there seemed to be an unspoken thing between them. Chavri decided she didn't care if it was spoken or not, so long as she could keep touching Stacia. It was the only thing that made everything that was happening feel real.

"Riku looks so much like Uncle Riska," Stacia said. "I mean, I know he's his great great grandfather, but seriously, they look like brothers. And how weird is it that he's my great great grand-nephew?"

"Weird," Chavri said. "And I know the feeling."

"And Prince Ardan's eyes—that Aisling blue eye thing is powerful," she said.

"Except it skipped me," Chavri said.

"Blue eyes are overrated," Stacia said, and smiled at Chavri. Chavri squeezed her hand.

"So, it's just the three of us. We're the only ones left from our time." Stacia snuggled in closer to Chavri. The cramped space helped that, kept her from accidentally floating away, which had happened once before when she tried to give Chavri a hug and bounced off.

"And we're stuck on a Mehmtokian spaceship two days from L'Mondeau," Chavri said.

"And the mission is still to get on *Aurora One*," Lysa added. The three women looked at each other and then broke into a fit of laughter.

"Ye gods," Lysa said, wiping tears from her eye. "The more things change…."

"At least this time we're not going," Stacia said. This had been a point of contention between Chavri and Prince Ardan, as Chavri felt like after what she was able to do on *Aurora Three*, she should be allowed to go to *Aurora One*. But the prince had been adamant that she had risked her life more than enough. When Stacia agreed, Chavri relented.

"I wish no one would have to go," Lysa said. "I really feel like that ship has taken enough from Moarga."

"But there are ten people on it," Chavri said. "And if the spores froze and preserved us, there's a good chance the crew of the *Aurora One* can be saved too. Besides—the *Prestige* is really only equipped to handle eight people. They used up a lot of air while trying to save us from *Aurora Three*. There is not enough left for all of us to get home. We need the air tanks from *Aurora One*."

"And if there is any chance that ship can be started up again…." Stacia trailed off, but they were all thinking the same thing—they could take it home. Chavri wasn't sure if there was an official plan, but in her mind all the Moargans would get on the *Aurora One*, and the Mehmtokians would stay on the *Prestige*, and then she wouldn't have to deal with Declan anymore. He had been filled with questions about her time, and had told her horrible stories about the prince the Mehmtokians had been trying to convince her parents to marry her off to. Chavri didn't like to think her parents would have gone through with it, but she had no real way of knowing that. Still, she lamented the fact that her disappearance removed even that option, and that when war with The Thirteenth was declared, they didn't have the benefit of a strong alliance with Mehmtok.

The only good thing about Declan's constant talking was that he gave as much information as he asked for.

"We should probably go out there," Lysa said. "I'm taking over for Eural on the bridge. Prince Ardan believes, and I agree, that it's better to keep one Moargan there at all times."

Chavri nodded. Part of her was glad that the prince shared her mistrust of the Mehmtokians, and part of her wished that she had just been overreacting.

"I want to stay on coms with Riku," Chavri said. "I still can't believe he's going, or that Ardan is letting him go."

"He's the highest ranked guard here," Lysa said with a shrug. "His injuries are minor, and he has experience with the hyphae. He's ideal for the mission."

"Spoken like a true guard," Stacia said with a sigh. "You sounded just like Riska then."

"He trained me well," Lysa said.

They all became quiet then.

"I keep thinking about him, sending us off from the Moargan Command Center. He never did that before."

"I think about that too," Lysa said.

"He probably never forgave himself for letting us go."

"Probably not," Lysa said.

Chavri hugged Stacia closer.

"We have a lot to make up for," she said. "I hope the *Aurora One* is worth it."

Chapter 25

Riku watched as Eural pulled herself along the rope connecting the *Prestige* to the *Aurora One* and was very glad that this time he wasn't going to face the fungus alone. Chavri had proven herself and done an incredible job saving everyone. But she wasn't a soldier. Eural was efficient in her movements, and not the least bit sentimental about her mission.

Beside him in the *Aurora One* airlock, Dr. Bernard and Geoff watched Erual's progress. The two Mehmtokians looked so much alike in their suits that from behind Riku couldn't tell them apart until they spoke. Geoff almost never did speak—that was the difference.

This time they were going to approach the problem of the fungus differently. The main objective was to get the power on the *Aurora One* online. The secondary objective was to find and recover every body they could, finding and repairing the space suits to the best of their ability. Lastly, they were going to suck all the air out of the ship, and suck the hyphae out the airlock. They were each armed with fire extinguishers that had been modified to fire a more direct blast, the concentration and pressure great enough to get through a single hypha. Riku had given orders that no one would use Substance 248 without another standing guard.

Lysa was going to monitor the *Prestige* bridge. After a brief lesson, she was familiar with all the controls and proved to know even more about space flight than either Geoff or Eural. Since she was the pilot for the royal ship of Moarga, it made sense that she would have the most training and experience.

Riku was surprised at the doctor's desire to join the mission, but Dr. Bernard was anxious to see for himself if the fungus reacted the way Chavri reported. Riku suspected the doctor didn't believe the princess, but Riku did. He didn't plan on taking any chances.

As Eural completed her trek across the rope, Riku reached out a hand to pull her into the open airlock. She climbed inside and Riku pulled the external door closed.

He moved to the interior door while the airlock pressurized. It was much faster than on the *Aurora Three*, despite the fact that it was a lot bigger. The ship was a lot more advanced than the *Aurora Three* in general. From what Riku knew, the *Aurora One* had been the pride and joy of the Moarga province when it was commissioned. Queen Iris had been very interested in space flight and in exploring the solar system around L'Mondeau. The *Aurora One* was said to be the source of a lot of what the people of L'Mondeau knew about their solar system.

When the analogue meter indicated that the air pressure was stable, Riku opened the door.

The airlock emptied into an open space packed with equipment, including additional space suits. Dr. Bernard went to them immediately and took scans—or at least Riku assumed it was the doctor since Geoff hadn't seemed particularly interested in exploring anything. Stacia had done the same when she first explored the ship, but her scanners had been lost in engineering when she encountered the fungus.

"They are intact," Dr. Bernard said. "Everything here appears to be in order. But the atmosphere is not what it should be, drained of oxygen. I am surprised that there are no hyphae here."

"Both Stacia and Chavri said there weren't. This is a much larger ship than *Aurora Three*. It could be that the hyphae just didn't reach this far."

"Interesting," Dr. Bernard said. He didn't bother to tell Riku why that was interesting though.

"This way to engineering," Eural said, heading down a hallway. She had her own scanner out—no one wanted to be taken surprise by the fungus.

Riku had been examining a door in the other direction, trying to make sense of what his scans were telling him was beyond it. He made a mental note to talk to Ardan about the scans later and turned and followed Eural down the hall, staying close to her. Geoff and Dr. Bernard lagged some distance behind Riku and Eural—another conscious choice on the part of the team to ensure that the second team had enough warning to get out of the way of any danger the first team encountered.

They came into a sizeable area with tables that had been screwed into what Riku was thinking of as the floor. He thought there was something odd about them, but couldn't figure out what.

"Does this ship have artificial gravity?" Dr. Bernard asked. Riku turned back to the tables and noticed benches below them. For sitting. Which wasn't necessary in weightlessness.

"I guess so," Riku said. Suddenly the scans on his readout from earlier made sense—there were all sorts of strange machines in there, and he figured those machines created the artificial gravity.

"How?" Dr. Bernard asked.

"This was one of the first ships built by the colonists, and the Moargan royalty kept it up-to-date as much as they could. I know the colony ship had artificial gravity. I guess they figured out how to make it on other ships."

"This might be the smallest one they could put a system like that on," Eural said. "From what I remember of my training, it takes a certain mass size to make it effective."

"So, it's possible?" Dr. Bernard said. "Artificial gravity?"

"Dr. Haider would know better than me," Riku said. As they moved past the mess hall, they got to a junction with a ladder up and another down.

"Down," Eural said. She went down first, keeping one hand on the ladder and leading with her feet. Riku followed suit as soon as she was clear, knowing that Geoff and Dr. Bernard would wait a moment before following.

"It's another hallway," Riku said. He could see what looked like doors on either side and pulled his scanner out. There was open space behind the doors. "I think there are crew cabins down here," he said.

"I'm getting the same readings," Eural said. "Our path is forward though."

They came to another junction, this one with only one direction—down.

"We're close," Eural said. "Just down there."

"I'm picking up fungus readings ahead," Dr. Bernard said.

"In engineering," Riku said. "There's a ladder leading down.

Chavri said it was a short hallway, and the door to engineering was at the end of it. She said it was open, that there was a large hypha blocking it open."

"We have a plan," Dr. Bernard said. "Time to execute."

Riku turned to Eural, who had turned to look back at everyone, and nodded. She gave a thumbs-up sign, and then went down the ladder, opting to go head first, replacing her scanner with a wrench. They had become the weapon of choice for the Moargans.

Riku followed closely after, opting to go down feet first. Eural had cleared the bottom when he got down there, and he saw her paused in the hallway, clinging to the side to avoid the hypha. Riku positioned himself across from her and waited for the others to come down.

Once everyone was in the hallway, Riku signaled to Eural, and she moved through the doorway into engineering, carefully not making any contact with the fungus. She went to the right, and Riku followed her, both of them finding spots just inside the door to assess the situation, while Geoff and Dr. Bernard went to the other side of the door.

Riku was not prepared for the sight in front of him. Chavri and Stacia told him that engineering on *Aurora One* was a lot larger than on *Aurora Three*. But Riku thought you could probably put the entirety of *Aurora Three* in this room alone.

And hyphae were everywhere.

"We get the power on. We get the bodies, and we move them back to the mess hall, strap them down. We don't get pricked by anything," Eural said, reviewing their mission.

She headed for the nearest panel, and then made her way to everyone that wasn't covered in hyphae until she found the one she was looking for. She went to work, and soon after, lights came on throughout engineering. Riku let out a small cheer.

"Step one complete," Eural said, and Riku could hear the grin in her voice. "Step two bodies. We should make a chain."

"Agreed," Dr. Bernard said. "And I won't run any experiments until we get the crew safe."

Riku used his scanner to look for any human signs. He found one not too far away.

"There," he said.

"Got it," Eural said. She carefully moved the body away from nearby hyphae and passed it back to Riku. Riku in turn passed it back to Geoff, and in doing so noticed that the body was male, and wearing a baggy uniform that looked like was half a space suit, as though he'd taken a suit off down to his waist and stopped. The top part of it flopped against the man's hips. He was young, looked like he'd been strong. Riku silently wished the man luck and hoped he would make it.

The first five bodies were easy enough to spot and free, and were secured in the mess hall. Eural was having a harder time with body number six. It was a woman whose arm had been pierced by a spike, and Eural wasn't sure how best to get her off it.

"We yank the arm off, and then untangle her foot. We should be able to move her then," Riku said.

"Allow me to observe the wound," Dr. Bernard said, and Eural switched places with him so that he could get a better look. Geoff kept watch over the group, eyeing the hyphae with an air of boredom.

"The wound won't be fatal," Dr. Bernard said. He took a pair of clamps out of his pocket and gently put them on the spike under the woman's hand. He held the hypha with the clamps and pulled up on the woman's hand, effectively freeing her. Eural used her wrench to push away the hyphae near the woman's feet, and pretty soon she was being passed back to Riku, who passed her back to Geoff, who floated away with her back to the hallway.

After that Dr. Bernard was called in to inspect any wound, and his handy clamps—he had three different sizes—were utilized effectively. Only one person had something that could be a fatal wound, the tip of a hypha having impaled his stomach. Dr. Bernard personally escorted that one to the mess hall and wrapped the wound the best he could. It wasn't currently bleeding, but it would once the spores were killed off.

It was relatively quick work to patch up the various holes in the suits and to make sure that everyone would survive most any catastrophe that could befall *Aurora One*.

Then the group went back to engineering.

"The mycelium seems focused around that object, there in the middle. I'd like to free it," Dr. Bernard said. The object was in the center of the thickest cluster of hyphae, and Riku knew there was no way to free the object without at least cutting through some of them.

"It would be safer to suck it out into space with the fungus," Riku said.

"From what I can tell, that object is the source of the fungus growth. I think we should figure out what it is before we do anything to the fungus, don't you? Whatever it is, it could be valuable. Geoff will get it, won't you?" The doctor looked at Geoff for confirmation. Geoff shrugged.

"Tell me what you want me to do," he said.

It was quickly decided that Geoff would go in first and spray a generous amount of Substance 248 over the center of the object. Riku would watch Geoff's back, and pull him away from the area as soon as possible. Dr. Bernard thought that was overkill, but Riku took what Chavri described seriously. Eural would approach the object from the other direction and pull it free, handing it off to Dr. Bernard behind her, and then getting herself to safety as soon as possible. Again, Dr. Bernard thought Riku was overdoing it.

"It's a fungus. It has interesting growth patterns, but it is not a moving thing. It may respond to stimuli, but it can't think."

"We stick to the plan," Riku said.

Everyone got into position. Geoff took out a small tank filled with Substance 248 and aimed it at the center of the mass of hyphae. He turned the gas on.

Almost immediately the hyphae around the object began to wither and retreat. But in Riku's peripheral vision he saw a hypha rear up as if to strike. He yanked Geoff back and saw Eural pull the object toward her. All around them, the hyphae were moving, and Riku had to swat several spiked ends out of his way as he pulled Geoff back.

But Geoff was still spraying. The hyphae were moving rapidly toward him.

"Shut it off!" Riku yelled. Geoff didn't respond and Riku

reached around his body to get to the tank. It was only then that he saw the hypha sticking out of Geoff's neck, just below the edge of his helmet, the blood already frozen and covered in spores.

Riku knocked the tank out of Geoff's hand and continued to pull him back, yanking him off the end of the hypha.

"Get out of engineering!" he yelled and hoped that Eural and Dr. Bernard were still alive to hear him.

The tank that Geoff had been using was still on, and spinning wildly around the room. Every hypha the gas touched seemed to pull back, while other hyphae grew long and sharp toward the tank, spiked ends trying and failing to pierce the outside.

Riku got Geoff past the door and into the hallway, pushing him toward the ladder. He whirled then and went back inside, looking for Eural and Dr. Bernard. Eural had the doctor, who was moving at least and therefore likely not frozen, and was dragging him behind her. Riku reached out when she got close and helped pull her through the door.

Behind her was chaos of gas and hyphae.

"We have to depressurize the ship," she said. "We need to kill this thing, now!"

She shoved Dr. Bernard in front of her. He was holding the object that had been at the center of it all, a gold covered capsule about the length of an arm and the diameter of a large watermelon. His nose was bleeding, but he otherwise seemed all right.

"It hit him in the head," Eural explained to Riku as they made their way back to the ladder and up it. Dr. Bernard had gone first. "I guess I pulled too hard. His stabilizers didn't kick in fast enough."

Riku felt no sympathy for Dr. Bernard—Geoff was likely dead because of his insistence of getting the object.

Finally, everyone was back in the mess hall, and Dr. Bernard was looking at Geoff's open wound.

"I don't know that I can save him from this," he said. He seemed lost, still in shock that all his assertions that the fungus couldn't do all the things it did do were so wrong. His hands floated over Geoff without purpose or plan.

Eural scanned Geoff's body. "We'll have to worry about that later. Seal the suit and let's get going."

Dr. Bernard seemed reluctant to leave Geoff, and it redeemed him a little in Riku's eyes. He did insist on keeping the object with him, finding a large bag that would let him strap it to his back. Riku hoped the object was worth it.

The three of them made their way back through the ship to the first junction, going up toward the bridge.

The bridge was also larger than Riku expected, and Eural let out a whistle when she saw it. There were a few scattered lights on around the edges of the room, but the main panels were dark. The bridge comfortably sat six people, three seats positioned in front of primary control stations, and the other three in front of panels that Riku couldn't determine the purpose of.

"This was a research vessel," Eural said. "I think those were for various sensor scans, extra stuff, the kind of stuff that Dr. Haider would go nuts over." She ran her hand over those panels, but moved past them to the seat centermost on the bridge, facing a large window. She used the restraints to strap herself in. Riku took the seat to Eural's right and did the same, and after some hesitation, Dr. Bernard took a seat by one of the sensor panels, which had space in front of it to swing his bag with the object in front of him. His view was completely blocked and he looked ridiculous.

Eural went about flipping various switches. After flipping one, all the lights on all the panels lit up at once. Then they blinked off and came back on one-by-one, indicating that each system was coming back online.

"We have primary power!" Eural said. "And actually, we have a lot of power. More than enough fuel too. Lots of air. All the systems are in working order. Everything just went into sleep mode." She looked over several panels and tapped something into the keypad in front of her. "It's a failsafe. Every hour the ship looks for a code to be entered into, or else it goes into power save mode. This ship is smart!"

"Can we depressurize engineering?"

"Better do the whole ship," Dr. Bernard said. "Just in case. Including here."

Riku suspected the doctor believed Chavri's stories now.

Chapter 26

Getting the fungus off *Aurora One* after that was easy. The dried up hyphae offered no resistance as Riku and Eural threw them out the airlock, Riku taking a lot of satisfaction in watching them float away. Exploration of the ship revealed that it not only had artificial gravity, but it had a med bay and attached research lab, both of which could be completely sealed off from the rest of the ship with independent air sources.

After consultation with the *Prestige*, it was decided that they would try to revive the *Aurora One* crew in the med bay.

Everyone on the *Prestige* wanted to come over to see *Aurora One*, but Lysa agreed to stay on the *Prestige* to keep an eye on her while the rest went over to the much roomier Moargan craft.

Eural got the artificial gravity working, which was both a relief and entirely surreal. It wasn't as strong as planet gravity, but it was enough to let people walk around, and for dropped objects to actually drop. While Riku missed the ability to float everywhere, he appreciated being able to touch Ardan without accidentally pushing him away.

The gravity also made reviving the *Aurora One* crew much easier, as they stayed on the operating table in the med bay without having to be strapped down. One by one, they were de-spored, only the person impaled by the hypha not surviving the process. Geoff didn't make it either, though Dr. Bernard tried every heroic measure he could think of.

Declan opted to take Geoff's body home to Mehmtok where

he would get a lavish funeral.

Then the crew had to explain to nine people how they were out of their time, how everyone they knew back home was long dead. Chavri took the lead on this. She made a grand speech about survival, about starting over, and about not being alone in being out of time. Riku had been very impressed, and by the look on Ardan's face, he was too.

"What about the probe?" a man asked. He was the first body Riku had seen in engineering, Darin Song, and he was the chief engineer on the *Aurora One*.

"Gold covered object, about ye big?" Eural asked, miming the dimensions.

"Yes," a woman said. "It's vitally important."

"As far as we can tell, it's also the source of the fungus," Dr. Bernard said. "It was at the center of the mycelium."

"That's my fault," an older woman said. Her name was Madeline Ordonez, called Mad for short. She had spiky silver-gray hair and deep laugh lines around her brown eyes. She was the captain of the ship, and had been an officer in the Moargan navy before that. Riku had liked her right away.

"Only because you take the blame for anything that goes wrong, Captain," said another woman, Dr. Sherri Kirby, the chief medical officer. She was younger and thicker than the captain, and had a mass of soft brown curls forming a crown around her head and a smattering of dark brown freckles across her nose and cheeks. "We were all so excited about the probe, I didn't do a thorough enough scan for foreign particles."

"Yeah, but I was the one who brought it to engineering,"

Darin said.

Eural caught Riku's eye and grinned at him. Riku understood why—it was the same kind of conversations their unit had, everyone trying to take their share of the blame and sparing the others any guilt.

"You said it was a probe?" Dr. Haider asked, cutting to the point.

"Yes," Captain Ordonez said, looking around the gathered crew from the *Prestige*. "Please gods, tell me you didn't flush it out with the fungus."

"No," said Dr. Bernard, stepping forward and holding out the object. "But it cost a man's life. I hope it was worth it."

"It's from Earth," said the Captain. "Those are Alliance markings on the outside." There was silence in the room. "It's what we've all been looking for."

It didn't take long until they were all back in engineering, where Darin had been trying to plug the probe into a central line so that they could access the data inside of it. This time Dr. Haider, Dr. Bernard, and Dr. Kirby all did very thorough scans of every part of it. Dr. Bernard did a second check for spores, and was about to start a third when Dr. Haider pulled him away.

"It's safe," she told him.

"I just don't want to make any more mistakes," he said.

She nodded and gently led him away so that Darin and the other engineers could connect the probe back to the *Aurora One*.

When Darin got the probe plugged in he found a message file and played it.

"This is Earth colony Oster, seeking the lost colony ship

L'Mondeau. If you are receiving this, know that the Interplanetary Alliance is searching for you. This probe has been tracking its travel. If you have found it, you will have found a map to our colony, and can send your ship to us. If for some reason you cannot send your ship to us, program the probe to return to us with a message and we'll come to you. Instructions on accessing the probe systems will follow. The Interplanetary Alliance is awaiting your return. People of the colony ship L'Mondeau—you are not alone. "

Riku reached out and took Ardan's hand. He looked across the room and saw Chavri had taken Stacia's hand as well. Chavri had tears in her eyes, and Riku could understand why. In fact, there were very few dry eyes in the room as the message played on repeat, a litany of instructions for accessing various data following.

"L'Mondeau isn't alone anymore," Chavri said.

"It never was," Stacia responded. "It just had to be found."

PART VI:

The Ever After

Now, our story seems to show

That a century or so,

Late or early, matters not;

True love comes by fairy-lot.

Though philosophers may prate

How much wiser 'tis to wait,

Maids will be a-sighing still —

Young blood must when young blood will!

Charles Perrault, The Sleeping Beauty in the Wood

Chapter 27

It took two days to get both the *Prestige* and the *Aurora One* back to L'Mondeau.

It took three weeks before the *Aurora One* and her crew went back into space to send the probe back to the Oster colony and the Interplanetary Alliance. It took nearly twice that long before the crew began to feel like they could actually build a life on Moarga. Captain Ordonez helped create the newly formed L'Mondeau space program, a joint effort between all twelve provinces, and the *Aurora One* crew became leaders in the organization. Still, it would be years before they even began to deal with their collective grief.

It took several more weeks before Declan was able to get Mehmtok to agree to an alliance with Moarga. It took months before Dr. Bernard and Dr. Haider, working together as part of the new alliance between Mehmtok and Moarga, were able to use the spores to create an effective counter to Substance 248 without creating an ecological disaster. Within eighteen months, they had the inoculation that Dr. Bernard had been after. The war with The Thirteenth was all but over after that.

It took six weeks before Chavri was declared the official new heir to Moarga. And it took six months before Ardan proposed to Riku, and they began to plan their wedding together. It took the end of the war with The Thirteenth before the wedding could take place. They worked with Dr. Haider to help former Thirteenth members reintegrate into society.

It took three years for the ambassador ship from Oster to get to L'Mondeau. Soon after the spore technology made long-distance travel in space a lot more tolerable when they found a way to control the Aurora Fungus to create a safe cryogenic sleep.

But before all of that, and before Chavri and her consort produced an heir for Lysa to guard, Chavri was standing in the Moargan royal gardens for the first time in her life.

She had seen them from windows and on viewing screens, but she had never been allowed to visit them. They were too populated, too hard to guard. They had dangerous plants that could snag a suit or *dupatta*. They were not that nice anyway, she had been told, as though that was even remotely the point. By the time she was twelve, she had stopped asking about them.

Chavri imagined what her parents would think of her if they saw her then. She wondered if her mother would still hold all that tension and worry she'd carried since Chavri was born. She wondered if her father would pace back and forth like he did whenever Chavri pushed her bounds. She wondered if they, like her, would still be struggling with the idea of her cure.

But now, three days after returning from space, she was in the royal gardens. She was wearing a *dupatta*, a purple one with reddish tinge that seemed to change color from different angles. It had small clear beads woven throughout it, adding a touch of sparkle. Stacia said it looked like a night sky at dusk lit up with stars. It didn't have a force field. In fact, Chavri wasn't even wearing it over her face. But not wearing one at all felt wrong.

A breeze made the flowers nearest Chavri bend down, and she imagined for a moment they were bowing to her, giving her a royal welcome to the royal garden. She felt the wind brush the edges of her *dupatta* against her face, and closed her eyes against the tickle. Bright sunshine was warming her bare arms. Her toes wriggled in open-toe shoes. Every part of her felt open, and free.

"Isn't that a pretty sight?" Stacia said, walking down the cobble path toward her.

"The flowers?" Chavri asked.

"You, basking in the sun," Stacia said. Chavri grinned at her.

"I can't believe how long I went without it."

Stacia reached out her hand, and Chavri took it. Stacia's hand was soft, and small, and delicate, and Chavri reveled in the feel of it. Stacia pulled Chavri toward her, standing up on her tiptoes to get her face as close to Chavri's as possible without touching. Everything that she hadn't been able to put into words before was there in Stacia's face. She still hadn't been able to say what she felt, but she could see that Stacia felt the same.

"We should probably talk about this at some point," Stacia said. Her breath was warm and sweet against Chavri's lips.

"At some point," Chavri said. She pressed her forehead against Stacia's, not entirely sure what to do—she had never even dared hoped to have this, let alone more. Stacia took the lead then, pressing her lips against Chavri's softly, then harder.

The kiss was nothing like Chavri was expecting, the sensations coursing through her skin and nerves and even down to her feet shocking and delighting her. When Stacia pulled back, Chavri had to fight the urge to pull her back in for more.

"Was that all right?" Stacia asked.

Chavri nodded, knew she was grinning like an idiot, but didn't care.

"That was amazing," she said softly.

"Good," Stacia said. "Cuz we're going to be doing that a lot, if that's all right with you."

Chavri pressed her lips to Stacia's as a response. She felt Stacia's hands move up her arms and slide around behind her neck, holding her close.

It was the greatest thing Chavri had ever felt. She wrapped her arms around Stacia and kept kissing her. She wasn't sure if she was good at it yet, but she was willing to put in the practice.

Some things take time.

The End

WANT MORE FROM THE GALACTIC DREAMS UNIVERSE?

TAKE A SNEAK PEEK AT...

SOLDIER, Princess, REBEL SPY

by

Karen Harris Tully

Chapter 1:

MEILIN - REBEL STARSHIP HMS TEMERITY

"Wei!" the drill sergeant barked from across the training center of the Rebel cruiser, hidden behind the nearest rocky moon of colony planet, Lyric. All the trainees stopped and looked up from their workouts and wrestling matches, waiting for the officer to complete his order. Meilin too, paused in her sparring match with a new recruit and looked over at the shout of her name. Her opponent however, who was at least four times bigger than she was, did not, and backhanded her hard, right across the cheekbone. She fell to her knees. Damn, that would teach her to not take eyes off the new guy. She wiped blood from her nose.

"Ha! Told you losers I could take her in a fair fight," he crowed to the other trainees. "Look, I hit her so hard, her anti-rec screen is imprinted on my hand." He laughed and held up the back of his hand for the crowd to see the dark and light triangular patches she had painted unevenly across her cheeks that morning. Other swirls, spots, and thick lines obscured her features to the government's surveillance probes, though it should be unnecessary amidst the Rebels. She liked to stay in practice. Her dark straight hair, held a streak of blue hanging over one eye, completing her ever-changing look. No one ever truly knew what Wei Meilin looked like under the makeup, and she wanted to keep it that way.

She shook off the late hit and the room fell silent.

She had indeed promised this new recruit a fair fight, and fair was fair. From her position on her knees, she threw an uppercut, fast and hard into his man bits. He froze for a second before crumpling to the mat.

"Wei Meilin!" Sergeant Xiaobo yelled more insistently.

"Coming!" she yelled back. "Seriously? The *shinse* I have to put up with to kill the Empress," she grumbled, testing her cheek as she made her way through the silent Rebel trainees toward the officer.

But the guy on the mat wheezed after her. "You *biao-zi.*"

She stopped with a sigh, then whipped around and flicked her hand, her middle finger arcing a white-hot bolt of energy at him.

"There," she said to those surrounding the twitching new guy. "When he wakes up you can tell him he won." She endured a withering glare from Sergeant Xiaobo before he turned and led the way to the Commander's office. Well, no big loss there; Xiaobo had never liked her anyway. She waited outside while the Sergeant filled in the Commander.

"Wei Meilin, get in here!" Commander Zhang barked.

Meilin stepped inside and saluted her unforgiving CO. She'd been training tirelessly for six years now. She had been a scared, angry seventeen-year-old when she'd arrived. She was no longer scared, but she was still angry. She had learned to fight and to control her unique plague "Gift"—well most of the time—and she hoped she was finally about to get her long-awaited assignment. It was her dream to infiltrate the Royal guard in the moon palace, the Jewel of Gallaius, and oust corrupt Empress Ming-Zhu. She'd gladly give up her Gift to have her family back, but since that wasn't possible, she was more than ready to avenge their deaths.

"Meilin, you know we can't have you electrocuting the other trainees." The Commander seemed tired of reminding her.

"He'll be fine, Commander. Besides, you used to say I needed all the practice I could get."

The Commander pursed her lips and said wryly. "You've been all practiced up for a while now. And your time has finally come. The Rebellion is ready for the next step in our plan." The CO turned around to retrieve a com pad from the desk behind her.

Yes! Meilin pumped her fists silently and did a little jig in place. She froze again as the Commander turned back toward her, looking down at the com pad.

"You'll be infiltrating the palace—"

Yes! Yes, Yes, Yes! She was sooo ready to kick some Royal a—

"—as a princess candidate."

Her previously dancing insides froze. "A *what*?"

"A princess candidate. There is a call out for girls age eighteen to twenty-four with Royal bloodlines. It seems our dear Prince is looking for a bride."

"A bride! But Ma'am, I'm a soldier, not a princess. And besides, I don't have Royal blood," she felt a triumphant surge of relief, but it was short lived.

"Ah, but your new documents *say* that you do." The Commander pushed a file folder across the desk toward her. "A blood test showing two point four percent royalty from your great, great, grandfather. Who knew?" she shrugged sarcastically at the results of the fake blood test. "I know you've trained as a soldier, but this is too good a chance to pass up."

"But," Meilin was horrified, "I can't marry the Prince!" She remembered that pale, lazy, pretty boy from the vid feeds years ago when she'd still lived on her family's farm, and had still believed in fairy tales.

"And we don't need you to. I don't care if you say two words to him. Your assignment is to fit in enough to be able to move around the palace undetected. Your job will be to use your Gift to pre-charge and ready the EMP, the Electro-Mag Pulse bomb we are sneaking in prior to our invasion. You will be tasked with significant changes to its guidance system, as it will arrive on the Royal moon disguised as a present; fireworks from a generous loyal to celebrate the Prince's engagement. The Royals will launch the fireworks rocket the night of the Prince's engagement ball, when he announces his choice for princess. Our forces will arrive to stage our coup during the ensuing chaos. This is imperative, Meilin. Our coup is resting on your shoulders. So I need to know, can you pull this off?"

Meilin took a deep breath and straightened her shoulders. As long as she could get close to the Empress, she didn't care how. She'd prance through the palace buck naked if that's what it took.

"Count on me, Ma'am."

"Good. You'll go with Yun now." As if from nowhere, a lithe young woman with iridescent purple hair and bejeweled rainbow eyebrows appeared at her elbow with a nod to Meilin. "You need to look the part of a princess and she's in charge of making sure you do and providing support during your mission. Go. You don't have much time before your transport leaves tomorrow."

Meilin allowed the young woman to lead her, passing an older man on their way out the door. He was a big man, tall and rotund with ruddy skin, dressed in a politician's slick smile and a formal court suit. Meilin recognized him immediately as Governor Fong, the Crown appointed leader of Lyric. He held a fancy box that was already open with the top tucked under, revealing a pale blue, glowing fruit resting on padded folds of red velvet. She stared. What was *he* doing on the Rebel ship, bringing presents to Commander Zhang?

"My dear Commander!" he exclaimed, striding into her office. She accepted the box while making shooing motions at Meilin and Yun with one hand. The door shut as soon as they were over the threshold.

Count on me, Ma'am. Twelve hours later, she was fully regretting those words. She'd been plucked, lasered, and sand-blasted, wrapped, squeezed, and shaped, puttied, masked, stripped, and lacquered to within an inch of her sanity. Almost every bit of skin was hairless and polished to a high gloss shine. The only hair she'd been allowed to keep were her eyebrows and eyelashes, as she was told they were a mark of status where she was going, the Royal moon, the Jewel of Gallaius.

Under the domes of the Jewel, every bit of breathable air and drinkable water had to be manufactured, purified, and recirculated over and over, and so, cleanliness was the height of fashion. Every person on the Jewel scrubbed every bit of their skin daily, before it, and any hairs, could slough off and become dust to clog the filters, or worse, part of the air they all breathed. The only people allowed to grow real hair were the Empress and her son the Prince. Instead, small holograph emitters were worn atop the bare heads of the court, allowing them to wear the illusion of any hairstyle they wished, providing it didn't outshine the Empress.

Currently, Meilin was staring at herself in a mirror, without makeup for the first time in years. Her shiny scalp was striking, but what she really noticed was her resemblance to her beloved Grandmama, lost thankfully years before the plague ravaged her town and killed her parents. She was glad her grandparents had not lived to see their family unable to pay their full tithe to the Crown, and the Royals' response of withholding the cure.

She forced herself not to get lost in the past and instead looked at the rest of her reflection. She was wearing the most restrictive, constrictive dress in a horrid periwinkle color, and matching, ridiculous platform shoes that clunked hollowly as she walked. And her nails were painted. Pink. She tapped them on the control plate to change them to a deep blue with tiny sparkles that resembled the starry night sky, and then again, changing them to the exact golden yellow of the mulberry candies her family used to make for the palace. She left the color as a reminder.

She tottered up the transport ramp and collapsed onto a padded seat bench of the non-descript shuttle she'd be taking to Lyric and the princess candidate transport, and then on to the Royal moon. She stood back up and sneered at her reflection in the shuttle window. She looked like a Loyal. Only those with nothing to hide from the Crown's drones went around bare-faced. She straightened and practiced the stupid smile she thought a princess would wear. This was her assignment and she was determined to succeed.

But first, she had to learn to walk in these god-forsaken shoes.

GALACTIC DREAMS

2019

ABOUT THE AUTHOR

 J.M. Phillippe spent the early part of her life in the deserts of Santa Clarita, California where she learned about fire season and idolized She-Ra; her adolescent/young adult years in the evergreen Seattle suburbs where she gained an appreciation for walking in the rain and earned a degree in Journalism and Creative Writing; and her early twenties in Los Angeles where she tried to make a go of it as a freelance writer and thus learned a great deal about being an administrative assistant before ending up in public relations. Then she did the most LA thing she could think of — she moved across the country to go to graduate school in New York City. She has settled in Brooklyn, New York and became a licensed clinical social worker. She spends her free-time binge-watching quality TV, drinking cider with her amazing friends, and learning the art of radical self-acceptance, one day at a time.

OTHER WORKS BY J.M. PHILLIPPE

Perfect Likeness

FIND OUT MORE AT:

JMPhillippe.com